"Have you ever shaved a man?"

"What?" Cassie was thrown completely off balance. *Of course she'd never shaved a man.* "Only with cutthroat razors," she said acidly. "I'm not—"

"Yes, I know," Adam cut in dryly. "You're not a damn barber...."

"You don't want a secretary, you want a slave! Or a submissive little wifey to run around after you," she added bitingly.

Rosemary Gibson was born in Egypt. She spent the early part of her childhood in Greece and Vietnam, and now lives in the New Forest in England. She has had numerous jobs, ranging from working with handicapped children, collecting litter and pumping gas to being an airline ground hostess, but she always wanted to be a writer. She was lucky enough to have her first short story accepted eight years ago and now writes full-time. She enjoys swimming, playing field hockey, gardening and traveling.

NO TIES
Rosemary Gibson

Harlequin Books

TORONTO • NEW YORK • LONDON
AMSTERDAM • PARIS • SYDNEY • HAMBURG
STOCKHOLM • ATHENS • TOKYO • MILAN
MADRID • WARSAW • BUDAPEST • AUCKLAND

ISBN 0-373-03344-3

NO TIES

CHAPTER ONE

'WHAT have you got in there? The kitchen sink?' The coach driver retrieved the overflowing rucksack from the boot and staggered mockingly under the weight as he handed it to the slim, jean-clad girl with tousled red-gold hair waiting expectantly on the pavement behind him.

'Thanks,' Cassie Richardson grinned back at him, tugging a faded denim jacket over her scarlet sweater. She hoisted the backpack on to her shoulders with practised ease and, smiling up at the coach, waved goodbye to the plump elderly woman who had kept her supplied with peppermints and conversation on the journey down from London.

It was good to be back! A feeling of pleasurable anticipation welled up inside of her, banishing fatigue as she walked along the high street of the Hampshire country town. Nothing seemed to have changed much in the last ten months, she thought with satisfaction, passing the familiar shops, many of which were already festooned with Christmas decorations to herald the approaching festive season. It was odd, she reflected, pushing her cold hands into the pockets of her jacket, that despite her nomadic existence, that restlessness inside her that prevented her settling anywhere for long, she would hate to return and discover the place where she'd spent the latter half of her childhood and teenage years dramatically altered. Wherever she travelled, home would always be this small town, Mead Cottage . . . and Kate.

She glanced up at the clock on the church as she reached the market square. Only four o'clock and it was almost dark. It was beginning to drizzle and she increased her pace, deciding it wasn't worth stopping to fish out her lightweight waterproof from her back-pack. Impossible to think that less than forty-eight hours ago she'd been basking in the Australian sun. She turned left into a semi-residential, tree-lined street and stopped in front of a square red-brick house, the ground floor of which had been converted into office space. Crossing the small gravelled car park, Cassie reached the entrance, her physical discomfort momentarily forgotten as, grey eyes softening, she surveyed the gold lettering on the door. Richardson's Secretarial Agency. Nothing twee or ambiguous. The owner's surname and the function of the business. Direct and to the point. Just like Kate.

She slipped off the rucksack and, holding it carefully by the straps, pushed open the door and walked into the reception area, slightly surprised to find it deserted. Depositing her rucksack on a chair, she slipped off her wet jacket and started across the green carpet to the inner office and stopped as she heard the sound of a shrill voice coming from within. Definitely not her aunt's calm, sensible tones.

'I just walked out, Kate. I couldn't stand it another minute. He's not difficult...he's impossible...inhuman. I wouldn't go back to work for him if you paid me a million pounds!'

The door flew open, and a fair-haired girl burst out. She reached the outer door and then paused, glancing back over her shoulder towards Cassie.

'Don't, whatever you do, accept a job with Professor Merrick! He's the most...' Adjectives appearing to desert her, the girl let out a murderous scream and vanished.

Cassie grinned wryly. In her excited state the other girl obviously hadn't taken in her travel-worn, dishevelled appearance and was evidently under the impression that she was a prospective employee. And Professor Merrick, the evident cause of the girl's agitation, was, Cassie hazarded a guess, probably some ill-humoured elderly academic from the nearby university. Kate had mentioned in her last letter that she was providing an increasing number of secretarial staff for the university. The university where Cassie herself had been offered a place when she'd been eighteen. And turned it down.

'I just want a year off,' she'd explained to her aunt. 'Travel a bit before I continue with my studies.' She'd expected Kate to protest but, if not exactly approving, she'd offered no resistance, except for the one proviso that Cassie at least complete a crash secretarial course on leaving school.

Cassie pulled a wry face, her eyes clouding. Somehow that year's deferral from university had been extended to four. Perhaps this time she really would settle down, start thinking of a career and pursuing the necessary qualifications. The problem was, she enjoyed her present bohemian lifestyle. She might not have much in the way of material possessions, but she had her freedom, wasn't tied down to any one place.

She placed a hand on the doorknob and hesitated. Perhaps she should have written to Kate and warned her of her impending arrival. Her aunt would undoubtedly be surprised to see her, but would she be pleased? For heaven's sake, Cassie chided herself as she remained uncertainly outside the door. She must be more jet-lagged than she realised to let those childhood insecurities start plaguing her after all these years. She was a grown woman now, not a nine-year-old child.

Silently she pushed open the door and stepped into the room, her eyes immediately drawn to the woman seated behind the desk. In her mid-thirties, dark hair drawn back in a neat chignon, clad in a severely tailored suit, she emitted an aura of brisk efficiency. Kate Richardson. Not just her aunt, Cassie thought with a rush of affection, but for the last thirteen years surrogate mother, sister, friend, all rolled into one.

'Hello, Auntie,' Cassie murmured in a mock-sugary voice.

The older woman lifted her head from the stack of paper in front of her and slowly rose to her feet. 'Hello, Niece,' she returned drily, but her dark brown eyes smiled, lighting up with warmth.

'You look frozen... Oh, Cass, bare feet and open sandals in December...'

'Haven't any winter shoes.' Cassie shrugged dismissively. How characteristic of her aunt not to demand immediately an explanation for her unexpected arrival but simply accept it, to act as if it were days rather than nearly a year since they'd last seen each other. Did anything ever throw Kate, send her into a panic?

'I caught an earlier flight.' That was something of an understatement. Two months earlier, to be exact. She'd originally planned to return to England in February when her year's work permit expired. 'It was just with Christmas coming...' She'd become homesick, she admitted. So much for her conviction that she was completely self-sufficient. She longed just to cross the room and hug her aunt, but Kate had never been demonstrative and she restrained herself.

'Your hair...'

'More practical. It was so hot...' Cassie ran a hand through the damp, tumbled red curls. She still felt a pang when she thought of her thick, waist-length tresses, completely unaware of how much the short, gamine style in fact suited her, emphasising the high cheekbones and delicate bone structure, the clear, candid grey eyes and generously curved mouth. She started to speak again but her words were muffled by a huge yawn.

'You must be exhausted. Are you hungry or would you just like to crash out?' Kate closed the file on her desk. 'I was going to have a chop for supper. I'll nip out and buy another one before the shops close. Why don't you go on up and have a bath?'

Cassie nodded, the thought of a long, hot soak infinitely appealing, if she could stay awake that long. She suddenly felt quite sick with tiredness. There was so much she wanted to tell Kate, so many questions to ask, ten months to catch up on... but it was simply too much effort right now.

'We'll talk tomorrow,' Kate murmured quietly. 'Go on up to the flat.'

'Don't worry about the chop... It's pouring with rain...'

Kate removed a mackintosh from a small closet and slipped it over her suit. 'I want to post some letters anyway.'

'What about the office?' Cassie queried. 'Where's Mary?' she added, referring to the middle-aged woman who acted as Kate's receptionist. 'She's not left?'

'Flu,' Kate answered laconically, fastening the belt around her waist. 'Half the girls are down with it right now.'

'I'll wait here until you get back.' Cassie moved to the radiator and warmed her hands.

'No need. I haven't any more appointments today so I'll lock up behind me.' Kate picked up an umbrella, swung her handbag over her shoulder and walked briskly from the room.

Retrieving her backpack from the reception area, Cassie returned to her aunt's office and, opening the connecting door, walked into the hall and up the narrow flight of stairs, bounding up the last few steps as she heard the insistent clamour of the telephone.

Flicking on the landing light, she picked up the office extension from the table.

'Miss Richardson?' enquired a curt male voice before she even had time to speak.

'Yes,' she agreed unthinkingly, grinning delightedly at the tortoiseshell cat curled up on the carpet near her feet. 'Tilly,' she mouthed at it, clicking encouraging fingers.

'Adam Merrick.'

Cassie's fair eyebrows knitted across her forehead, her mind dulled through lack of sleep. Merrick... Merrick... Of course, the impossible professor. And not in the sun-

niest of moods judging by the timbre of the deep voice.
He didn't sound quite as old as her mental picture of
him either, but then the telephone often distorted voices.

'I think I may be under some misapprehension, Miss
Richardson.' His voice was controlled, but there was no
mistaking the anger in it. 'Rather naïvely, I assumed that
your agency was in the business of supplying efficient,
competent secretarial staff. I didn't realise that in actual
fact you were running a programme of occupational
therapy for love-lorn females.'

Cassie rubbed the back of her hand across her weary
eyes. Oh, Lord, a comedian. 'Professor Merrick,' she
began firmly, but he ignored the interruption.

'Might I make a suggestion? Perhaps rather than
sighing and gazing out of the window all day, these poor
afflicted girls might find it more therapeutic to undertake
a short course in basic English grammar. Those who
complete the course might even be presented with a
dictionary.'

The arrogant, smug, sarcastic… Unsuccessfully Cassie
tried to camouflage a huge yawn.

There was a short abrupt pause.

'Am I boring you?'

Don't tempt me, Cassie thought silently, choking back
the affirmative. Dearly as she wanted to rush to the
agency's defence, and, obnoxious as this man sounded,
he was one of Kate's clients and it wouldn't be diplomatic to offend him. Besides, the agency wasn't her
province and she had no right to interfere. Best to let
Kate deal with the charming professor. At least he'd
stopped talking for a second and she might get a word
in edgeways and explain that she wasn't the right Miss
Richardson.

'Actually I'm——' she began, and wrinkled her
freckled nose with exasperation as the male voice over-
rode hers.

'I really don't have the time to listen to apologies or
excuses. However, for the sake of expediency and much

against my better judgement, I'm prepared to give your agency another chance. I'll expect someone tomorrow morning. Nine o'clock sharp. Good afternoon, Miss Richardson.'

'I'm not——' Cassie snorted inelegantly as the line was disconnected. Didn't Adam Merrick ever stop to listen to anything but his own voice? He was prepared to give the agency another chance. How gracious of him... What unbelievable largesse... Replacing the receiver, she dismissed the professor from her mind and continued down the landing to her bedroom.

Crossing the oatmeal carpet, she gazed out of the window that overlooked the small back garden. In the distance, just visible in the deepening gloom, lay the river meads from which the name of the house originated. In the summer the meadows were dotted with wild flowers. Tonight they were covered in puddles of water and Cassie knew that if the rain persisted all night by the morning she would look out on to a lake.

She drew the chintz curtains together and turned around, warm contentment seeping through her as she surveyed the familiar gold and cream room. Bookshelves ran the length of one wall. She'd never been able to discard a book, still possessed the illustrated fairy-stories of her infancy. Outdated school textbooks, shabby, worn children's books vied for space with adult popular fiction and the well-known classics in a disorderly confusion. One day, Cassie vowed, she would sort them out, arrange them in some sort of order.

A map of the world, dotted with coloured drawing pins, dominated the opposite wall. Yellow pins marked her progress through America where she'd spent one summer working on a children's holiday camp before exploring the vast country by Greyhound bus in the fall. The blue pins were reserved for Europe. Switzerland where she'd worked as a chalet maid...France where she'd gone grape-picking...Italy...Spain. Never staying anywhere long enough to become too attached to any one place—or person.

Stripping off her clothes, she removed a towelling robe from the pine wardrobe and wrapped it around her slight body. She would unpack properly tomorrow, she decided, sitting down on the edge of the bed with the rucksack between her knees. Tonight she just wanted her toiletries and the present she'd bought for Kate. She fished out her washbag and then retrieved the waterproof pouch in which she kept her valuables. Unzipping it, she spilled the contents on to the bed. Passport, money, the black opal necklace from Coober Pedy for Kate, and a small framed snapshot of her parents.

She looked down at the two smiling faces and then carefully placed the photograph on her bedside table. Time had dulled the grief and she no longer missed her parents with that stabbing, agonising pain. Her feelings had become more objective. The man and woman involved in that fatal car accident hadn't simply been her mother and father—but two human beings who'd lost their lives at a tragically young age. It was their loss as much as her own that she now mourned.

Cassie flopped back on the bed and stared up at the white ceiling. Sometimes it troubled her that without the photograph she might forget what her parents had even looked like. She could no longer remember the sound of their voices, couldn't visualise the expressions on their faces.

She'd been nine years old when they'd been killed ... Why could she think of her parents' death with relative equanimity and yet still find it so difficult to think about ... ? Of course she shouldn't have eavesdropped ... shouldn't have been listening outside the dining-room door that afternoon thirteen years ago. But she'd known that the family conference held a week after the funeral had been called to discuss her future ...

*   *   *

'If only we hadn't planned that round-the-world trip. I suppose we could cancel it...' Her beloved grandmother, who knitted her jumpers, made her favourite chocolate cake. 'But I really do think Cassie would be happier with someone younger.'

'She needs a woman's influence.' Uncle George, who gave her piggy-back rides. 'It would be different if I were married... I suppose I could employ a housekeeper...'

'With the baby due next month and the twins not even three and Alan away so much on business trips, I just don't see how I can manage with another child...' Auntie Jean, who let her help bath Rupert and Mary.

'I think the best solution would be a boarding school. She would be with children of her own age. And we could all take turns to have her in the holidays.' Uncle John, who'd taught her to ride a bicycle.

Even now Cassie could recall the black, swirling shroud of shock and bewilderment that had engulfed her. Next to her parents, she'd loved these people more than anyone in the world, had thought they loved her. And not one of them wanted her. Well, she didn't care. She didn't need anyone. She wasn't going to cry...

'Cassie can live with me.' The quietly spoken words had slowly penetrated into her head.

'But, Kate, be sensible. What about your career? And a London high-rise apartment isn't the most ideal place for a child...'

But Kate hadn't been dissuaded by the rest of her family. She'd given up her prestigious job as PA to the chairman of a large pharmaceutical company, sold her flat, moved to Hampshire and set up the agency... and provided a home for her small niece.

Cassie's eyes flickered open. She was momentarily disorientated in the darkness and then stretched out a hand and switched on her bedside lamp. Kate must have come in, found her asleep and covered her with a duvet. She glanced at her wristwatch. Six o'clock. So she'd only been asleep for just over an hour.

Swinging her legs out of bed, she tightened the belt of her robe around her waist and padded from the room, frowning as she discovered the flat dark and silent with no sign of her aunt. Realisation dawned. She'd slept the clock round. It was six o'clock in the morning!

She crept quietly along the landing to the kitchen, anxious not to disturb her aunt. She'd make a cup of tea and then she'd have that long overdue bath.

Filling up the kettle, she plugged it in and took a mug out from the wall cupboard. The tortoiseshell cat emerged from the linen cupboard in the corner and began to rub itself around her legs, demanding breakfast with a vociferous mew.

'Morning, Cass.'

Cassie turned round and saw her aunt standing in the doorway, long dark hair loose around her shoulders. 'Oh, Kate, I'm sorry. Did I wake you?'

'I was awake anyway.' Kate placed another mug on the table. 'Sleep well?'

'Like a log.' Cassie filled up the teapot with boiling water and clamped a hand to her forehead. 'Oh, heavens, I've just remembered. Professor Merrick phoned when you were at the shops yesterday. He thought I was you and didn't give me a chance to tell him otherwise. I should have left a note...'

'Not to worry,' Kate murmured peacefully, opening the fridge to retrieve the milk jug. 'I should have phoned him myself yesterday really, but I wanted to wait until I had a chance to talk to Julia calmly and find out exactly what all the fuss was about. I couldn't get much sense out of her yesterday.' She poured out the tea and sat down. 'So what did he say?'

Pulling a face, Cassie gave her aunt a brief resumé of her conversation with Adam Merrick and then grinned. 'Put him on the black list,' she suggested.

Kate took a sip from her mug. 'He might have some justification for his complaint,' she admitted slowly. 'Julia's usually extremely competent, but she split up with her fiancé last week and she's a bit fragile right now. I had her covering in reception the last couple of days.' She sighed and swept back her luxuriant dark hair. 'I shouldn't really have sent her to the professor's but with most of the girls down with this flu virus I simply didn't have anyone else and Julia assured me she was back on an even keel.'

'So what about today? He's expecting someone at nine.'

Kate shrugged. 'I'll just have to call him and tell him I don't have anyone available. I'll lose him as a client but it can't be helped.'

Cassie wasn't fooled by the casual shrug. 'Would that matter a lot?'

'Not directly, I suppose,' Kate admitted. 'This is the first time he's used the agency so he's not exactly a regular. But he's a history lecturer at the university so I might lose other potential clients if the word gets round that the agency is unreliable.'

So she'd been right in her original assumption that Adam Merrick was part of the university faculty. She could just imagine him lecturing, revelling in the sound of his own pedantic voice, withering with acid sarcasm any student who had the temerity to interrupt. 'What exactly does he need a secretary for?' Cassie asked. 'Isn't it the vacation now, anyway?'

'He's writing a book.'

No doubt some long-winded, humourless historical tome which he planned to inflict on future generations of students. 'Why doesn't he just write it out longhand and have it typed up when he's finished?'

'I suppose he finds it easier to dictate.'

More likely wanted an admiring audience to hang on to his every word, Cassie thought silently. Oh, well, it wouldn't kill her to humour him for a couple of days until Kate had someone else available. 'I'll go if you like.'

Kate studied her thoughtfully. 'Sure?'

Cassie nodded.

'OK. Thanks.'

Cassie smiled down into her cup of tea. Kate never wasted time with platitudes, never fussed, knew that she wouldn't have made the offer if she hadn't meant it. 'Where does he live? At the university?'

'No. In one of the cottages just along the lane from Richard. He moved there a couple of months ago when he took up his post at the university. I've never actually met him in person, just spoken to him on the phone, so I don't know a lot about him.'

She'd doubtless checked out the good professor with the forgiving nature through the university though, Cassie surmised, because Kate would never allow any of her female staff to go to an isolated cottage without checking that the client was *bona fide* first. 'So how is Richard?' Kate hadn't mentioned him at all in her last few letters which had made her wonder... 'Still see him?'

'From time to time.' Kate smiled, but her niece saw the shadow in her expressive eyes. Richard Fielding, Cassie thought privately, needed a bomb put under him. Maybe that would bring him to his senses and stop him taking Kate for granted. It would serve him right if Kate fell madly in love with someone else and he lost her for good. She sensed Kate watching her and looked up.

'It's nice to have you home, Cass. I've missed you.'

Cassie felt a warm glow tingle through her. She knew how difficult her aunt found it to express her feelings. Perhaps that was half the problem with Richard. 'It's good to be back,' she returned lightly. It had never occurred to her that Kate might actually miss her, might actually be lonely at times... Hell, she was selfish. At twenty-two, Kate had changed her whole life because of her. And what had she done to repay her? Gone swanning off around the world as she soon as she could.

'Another cup?'

'Mmm. Thanks,' Cassie murmured absently. 'Kate?'

'Yes?'

'Um. Nothing.' With sudden awkwardness Cassie pushed her mug across the table to be refilled. It wasn't Kate who found difficulty in expressing her feelings or showing affection, she recognised with a jolt. It was her. She was spontaneous, totally natural and at ease with people she barely knew, yet as soon as she started to care about anyone that familiar, constraining knot started to form deep inside her and grow tighter and tighter. She became flip, over-casual. There had been that Welsh boy she'd met at the backpackers' hostel soon after her arrival in Australia. She'd been grateful to him for showing her the ropes, enjoyed his company, enjoyed his undemanding kisses. She'd liked him. A lot. So why hadn't she even given the relationship a proper chance? Why had she immediately backed off the moment she'd sensed that he wanted more than merely a light-hearted romantic friendship? Because she simply wasn't ready to settle down yet, wasn't ready for a serious long-term relationship. That was all. Perfectly normal at her age, surely? Abruptly she picked up her replenished mug and drank her tea swiftly, ignoring the niggling feeling at the back of her mind.

It was starting to sleet as Cassie drew up on the grass verge outside the red-brick cottage. Surrounded on two sides by arable land and on the third by a copse of trees, its nearest neighbour was the farm she had just passed back down the lane.

Locking the door of Kate's saloon car behind her, Cassie pulled the hood of her grey duffel coat over her red curls and, frowning with concentration, carefully picked her way up the paved path to the front door. The navy blue court shoes that toned in with the skirt and jumper borrowed from Kate weren't high by any means,

but after wearing flat sandals for so long it was difficult
to adjust to walking in heels again.

Reaching the protection of the porch, Cassie rang the
bell, heard the sound of a dog barking from inside and
half turned to survey the front garden with its profusion
of rose-bushes and trees. It would be glorious in the
summer, a riot of colours and scents, she mused, and
smiled. Having only lived here a couple of months, the
professor was obviously not responsible for the well es-
tablished garden, but perhaps it had influenced his decision to purchase the secluded cottage. He was probably
nearing retirement, planned to spend his leisurely days
pottering among the roses, lovingly cultivating prize
specimens to be entered into local horticultural shows.
Julia, her predecessor, had doubtless been over-sensitive
yesterday. The elderly academic was probably a real
sweetie—and just happened to have an unfortunate telephone manner.

The door opened and Cassie was taken aback to find
herself being studied by a pair of solemn blue eyes set
in a small face. She'd been convinced that the professor
was a confirmed bachelor, hadn't for one moment supposed that he might actually be married, have a family.
But surely this boy, who only looked about five, would
be far too young to be his son. Grandson?

'Hello. Are you a taxi?' the boy enquired gravely,
carefully fastening the buttons on his school coat.

'No,' Cassie returned with equal gravity. He looked
so incredibly adorable with that small cap on his head.
'I'm a girl.' Her mouth curved as the small boy burst
into a delighted chuckle, the flippant remark evidently
appealing to his sense of humour. 'Would you tell your
grand...Professor Merrick that I'm here?'

'He's just coming.' As he reached the last button on
his coat and found no opposing button-hole, the boy
frowned.

'You've missed one at the top.' Instinctively, Cassie
stooped down and refastened his coat.

'Thank you.' The boy surveyed her seriously, his face on a level with her own. 'I've a wobbly tooth,' he confessed nonchalantly. Opening his mouth wide, he invited her inspection and seemed pleased by her expressions of admiration.

Lips twitching, Cassie straightened up and stiffened as she saw the figure looming in the doorway, a large shaggy black dog at his heels. Engrossed in her small, endearing companion, she hadn't heard him approach, wondered how long he'd been standing there watching her. The waxed jacket encasing the powerful shoulders was unfastened, revealing a green cashmere sweater and close-fitting navy denims that clung to muscular thighs and long, lean legs.

Irritated by the sudden unwelcome dryness in her throat, Cassie tilted her head upwards and received a brief impression of blue unsmiling eyes, and hard, uncompromisingly male features. Stubble as dark as the unruly hair covered the lower half of his jaw but did little to disguise or soften the square, tenacious chin and firm, straight mouth. Her nostrils were assailed by the smell of soap. He must have woken late, simply had time to shower and throw on some clothes...

'Professor Merrick?' she enquired with a brisk, confident smile that belied her growing unease and, on receiving a curt affirmative nod slowly held out a clammy hand, trying to mask the dismay on her face. This man towering over her could not be Professor Merrick. For some irrational, illogical reason she refused to accept his identity, clung on to her mental picture of the rose-loving elderly academic with the proverbial heart of gold. He was several decades too young for a start—somewhere in his mid-thirties—and he had the hard, rugged appearance of a man who worked out of doors, engaged in some sort of physical activity, not one who must surely spend a large part of the day behind a desk. He could not possibly be Adam Merrick. The denial whipped through her mind again. She did not want to spend up to eight hours a day in close proximity with this man, shied away from the thought with an intensity that shook her profoundly.

He ignored her outstretched hand. 'You're late.' The deep voice was unnervingly familiar, destroyed any last vestige of hope, and brought her back to her senses with a jolt, her hackles rising instantly to the cold, accusatory remark.

She most certainly was not late. She had deliberately allowed plenty of time for the journey, and a swift glance at her wristwatch confirmed that she was ten minutes early. Her exasperation changed to incomprehension as, without a word, Adam Merrick slammed the front door behind him and guided the young boy ahead of him towards Kate's car.

'Professor Merrick...' Cassie tottered after him. Damn these shoes. Why didn't the infuriating man ever listen? She might have been wrong about his physical appearance but her original snap assessment of his character yesterday was unfortunately proving to be all too accurate. 'I'm not——'

'Well, don't just stand there, for Pete's sake.' He cut through her protest, surveying her impatiently over the roof of the saloon. 'Unlock the doors.' The small boy tugged at his sleeve for attention. 'Yes, William?'

Cassie was startled by the change in his manner and voice as he glanced down at the child. All signs of impatience were eradicated.

'I think that's the taxi.'

Adam Merrick glanced down the lane and saw the approaching black car, the golden logo on its doors advertising a local taxi firm. 'Hmm.' He faced Cassie again. 'So you must be from the agency. Why did you go through this ridiculous charade instead of introducing yourself straight away?' As he spoke, he moved around the side of the car and stood towering above her, directing the full force of his brilliant blue eyes on to her upturned face.

'Here.' He extracted a set of keys from his pocket and held them out to her. As she reached to take hold of them, Cassie was disconcerted to discover how instantly aware she was of the lean fingers brushing fleetingly against her outstretched palm. The physical contact was minimal, almost non-existent and yet her hand was tingling, warmth shooting up her arm in tiny little shock-waves.

'I'll be back when I've dropped William off at school.' The already deep-timbred voice seemed to have dropped a further octave and his eyebrows were knitted across his forehead in a dark, forbidding line. 'Go and wait in the house.'

Cassie's stomach muscles tensed as he glowered down at her. She could feel the hostility radiating from his body, could see it reflected in the dark shadowy depths of his eyes. How could she possibly have aroused such a degree of antipathy in a virtual stranger, someone with whom she'd barely exchanged two words?

'Have an early coffee-break. Polish your nails. Dream about your boyfriend. Read your magazine. Get it all over and done with in your time and not mine.'

Cassie's muscles relaxed, her mouth beginning to curve. So she'd completely misjudged him. He had a sense of humour after all. He was teasing her, depicting the vacuous dumb blonde secretary so beloved by writers of television comedies. The smile froze on her lips as she encountered the cold, stony gaze, the chilling un-responsive face that looked as it had been carved out of granite. My God, he was serious...meant every damn word...

Before she had time think about retaliating, he turned and strode towards the taxi leaving Cassie gazing after his tall, retreating figure with a mixture of anger and stunned disbelief. He was the most appallingly rude man she had ever encountered in her life—an arrogant, ill-mannered, intellectual snob. No wonder he required a temporary secretary—no one in their right mind would work for him on a permanent basis, would tolerate being treated like a mindless bimbo. Julia had doubtless been one in a long line of secretaries to walk out on him.

She surveyed Kate's car with narrowed eyes. Why should she be subjected to this man's rudeness for even a day, even an hour? She had every justification for leaping in the car right this minute and speeding back to Mead Cottage. Her aunt would surely understand and sympathise when she explained just how obnoxious was Adam Merrick. Huh. He'd probably only contacted Kate's agency because he'd already been blacklisted by all the others in the locality. Every instinct in her being urged Cassie to get into the car and go.

She scowled, her eyes darkening uneasily. She just couldn't shake off that feeling almost of foreboding curdling deep inside her, was uncomfortably aware that her urgent desire to escape had nothing to do with her prospective employer's abrasive manner but something far more intangible.

Oh, for heaven's sake, she chided herself mentally. She wasn't some timid school-leaver, to be reduced to a blubbering, nervous mass of jelly by a few caustic words. Her lips compressed together resolutely. The thought of rushing back to Kate, admitting failure, letting down the agency, was inconceivable. Confidence surged back through her; the fleeting moment of near-panic now seeming laughable. She wasn't going to be intimidated by some dictatorial, domineering chauvinistic male— could certainly deal with the Adam Merricks of this world. Closeted in his narrow world of academia, he'd obviously developed an over-inflated notion of his own importance, was doubtless far too used to having his students jump at his every command.

Turning her back deliberately on Kate's car, Cassie walked swiftly and purposefully back up the path to the cottage. She wasn't going to run away from or kow-tow to any man. And that included Professor Adam Merrick!

CHAPTER TWO

HER chin set at a resolute angle, Cassie inserted the key into the front door. Adam Merrick hadn't asked for any identification, hadn't even waited for her to confirm that she was from the agency, simply handed over his keys to a total stranger. She might be a hardened criminal, a robber, an arsonist... Why hadn't he driven his son to school himself? She'd glimpsed a red car through the open door of the garage when she first arrived. And where was his wife?

As she pushed open the door, the black dog tore by her and sped into the garden. Damn. 'Here, boy...girl. Dog!' she called after it hopefully and, pursing her lips together, tried in vain to give an authoritative whistle. 'You'll get wet,' she cautioned.

Ignoring her completely, the dog crouched by the closed gate and gazed down the lane with wistful brown eyes.

So what was she supposed to do now, Cassie wondered exasperatedly? Forcibly drag that huge, shaggy canine protestingly back into the house? Some hope. Sighing sadly at the creature's misguided devotion, Cassie stepped over the threshold into a long narrow hall. Muddy paw marks and small footprints dotted the polished, red-tiled floor. A pile of old newspapers was stacked untidily in a corner next to an assortment of wellington boots. She raised her fair eyebrows. Unless she was very much mistaken, all those boots were for left feet...so where were the right feet?

A child's brightly coloured anorak, a large oiled sweater and a man's dark overcoat were hung on a row of pegs. No signs of any female outdoor garb, she noted, and grinned. No indication as to whether Mrs Adam

24

Merrick's taste in rainwear was as undiscerning as her taste in men. There were some women, she supposed grudgingly, who might find Adam Merrick's blatant masculinity attractive, regard it as an open challenge to their own femininity, but thankfully she didn't include herself among their number. Such obvious arrogant male machismo left her cold. Her initial reaction to Professor Merrick, she decided coolly, had been purely one of surprise.

Slipping off her duffel coat, Cassie hung it up on one of the pegs. She absently finger-combed her silky red hair into place, tucking an errant curl behind her ear, and then, guided by the smell of burnt toast, she walked slowly along the unfurnished hall. The unadorned walls on each side of her would have benefited from a couple of pictures to relieve the huge expanse of cream that stretched up to the high ceiling, she decided critically, and pushed open the door at the far end.

For a moment she remained motionless, eyebrows knitting together as her eyes moved slowly around the large, farmhouse-style kitchen. Tidiness was evidently not one of the strongest characteristics of the Merrick family.

The sink and surrounding work-surface were cluttered with dirty crockery, remnants not just of a hasty breakfast but the previous evening's meal. A school blazer, a striped tie, newspapers, pens, books, a paintbox, occupied two of the pine chairs drawn up to the refectory table. Presumably the family had actually eaten breakfast standing up or in the dining-room, because the table itself was covered by a half-completed jigsaw. Or most of it was. A half-empty bottle of whisky, a glass by its side, stood on the edge of the table. Hmm. A residue from last night... or this morning...

Her eyes alighted on the solitary child's blue wellington boot standing for some unfathomable reason on the mantelpiece of the large open brick fireplace that dominated one side of the kitchen. Head on one side, she studied it with thoughtful grey eyes. Functional but not an object of great beauty. No accounting for tastes, she supposed, but personally it wouldn't have been her choice of decorative ornament. Grinning, she reached up on tiptoe to retrieve the small boot and carried it out into the hall, placing it with its counterpart by the front door. Bingo. A complete pair.

The peal of the telephone echoing through the silent house made her jump. Should she simply ignore it or take a message? It might help if she could even see where the damn telephone was. Probably hidden inside a wellington, she thought sourly, tracing the telephone flex.

'All right, all right, I'm coming,' she muttered, scattering newspapers all over the floor as she lunged beneath them and retrieved the telephone receiver.

'Hello, love.' A comfortable elderly male voice spoke in her ear. 'Would you tell the professor that Annie won't be in today. She's got it now. But Emily might be able to give him a few hours.'

'Er, yes, of course,' Cassie agreed, amusement and bewilderment vying for supremacy, and then before she had a chance to establish the identity of the caller the line went dead.

Returning to the kitchen, Cassie walked across to the window and stared out into the back garden, unconsciously drumming her fingers on the edge of the sink unit. How long was the flipping man going to be? The previous occupant had evidently concentrated all his energies on the front garden, she mused absently, surveying the large expanse of lawn, interspersed with gnarled old apple trees. An ideal garden for a small boy. Plenty of room to run around, trees to climb. Oh, for heaven's sake, hurry up, Professor. She turned away from the window, flopped down in a chair and then jumped to her feet again. Had that been the sound of a car drawing up? Her stomach muscles clenched together... Oh, God, this was ridiculous. She felt as edgy as if she were waiting to sit an exam...

Spotting the transistor radio on the cluttered sideboard, she walked over to it and switched it on. Anything to break this awful oppressive silence. Humming to the popular melody echoing around the kitchen, she turned around, drawing in a sharp breath as she saw the dark, unshaven face peering through the window trying to attract her attention.

Unlocking the back door, she flung it open. 'You could have given me a heart attack creeping up on me like that.'

'Don't be so melodramatic.' Adam Merrick strode by her impatiently. 'I've been knocking on the back door for the last couple of minutes. You had my keys, remember?' He shrugged off his jacket and slung it over a chair. 'If you hadn't been listening to that infernal row, you might have heard me.' Moving over to the radio he switched it off and swung back round.

The hitherto huge kitchen seemed to have diminished in size, shrunk to almost claustrophobic proportions, dominated by the male figure leaning against the dresser, arms folded across his deep, powerful chest. Droplets of water glistened in the thick dark hair.

As the blue indifferent gaze swept over her, absorbing every detail of her appearance without even a glimmer of interest, Cassie felt her hackles rise. Who the hell did he think he was, looking her over as if she were some sort of exhibit at a show—an exhibit that evidently lacked any of the attributes needed to hold his male attention...?

She pulled herself up sharply, irritated that Adam Merrick had managed even momentarily to prick her ego, shake her confidence in her own femininity. What was the matter with her, anyway? The last thing on earth she wanted was this obnoxious man to evince a personal interest in her. She raised her eyes to his face. 'There was a phone call while you were out,' she informed him crisply. 'I'm afraid I didn't have chance to find who from but——'

'A secretary who can't even take a simple telephone message!' The deep sarcastic voice broke through her explanation.

Cassie's eyes flashed. 'Annie's got it now and won't be in today,' she said icily.

'My housekeeper. Mrs Evans. Flu,' he grunted laconically.

Cassie wasn't surprised by the information. She'd suspected something of the sort. Just as she was beginning to suspect that there was no Mrs Adam Merrick in residence at present. The existence of a housekeeper, the general disorder, the lack of any female paraphernalia, made her increasingly certain that this was an all-male household. So was the professor divorced? Widowed? Or was his wife's absence merely temporary? Who cared?

'Damn.' Blue eyes moved around the kitchen encompassing the unwashed dishes and pile of shirts stacked in a laundry basket by an ironing board and then rested speculatively on Cassie.

He had to be joking! The unbelievable gall of the man! 'Sorry,' she smiled sweetly at him. 'It would ruin my nails.' Would it kill him to wash a few dishes, iron a few shirts himself? Her mouth tightened contemptuously. Was he one of those puerile men who took a pride in proclaiming themselves hopelessly incapable of performing the simplest of domestic chores, seeing it as some sort of declaration of their masculinity? For a fleeting second her eyes locked into the blue ones and her stomach dipped. She was way off the mark there. This arrogantly self-assured male wouldn't doubt his own sexuality for a moment, had no need to declare it so obviously. Maleness radiated from every pore in his being, suffused the air around him like a musk. No. Quite simply Adam Merrick was an out-and-out chauvinist—a woman's place in the kitchen and... Without warning, colour rushed into her face and she directed her gaze down at the floor. 'Emily can give you a few hours,' she muttered, memory jogged.

'Who the hell is Emily?'

Her head jerked up. 'How the hell should I know?' she flung back.

Brilliant blue eyes scoured her flushed face. 'I've always found aggression in a woman singularly unattractive and unfeminine,' the deep voice observed.

You'll have to do better than that, Professor! Cassie looked back at him with withering disdain. She wasn't going to fall into that little trap. Did the conceited, insufferable man think that she was even remotely interested in his opinion of her? And she wasn't aggressive, never lost her temper... Dammit, she would love to pick up one of those plates lying on the sink and hurl it at his smug, complacent head... She could just imagine the sort of women that would appeal to him— passive, servile, compliant...

'Where's Lisa?'

'Uh?' She looked at him blankly for a moment. 'Oh, the dog. She went outside.' Surely he must have seen her when he arrived back at the cottage? She groaned inwardly. Perhaps the shaggy beast had become bored waiting for her master to return and wandered off, escaped through some gap in the garden hedge, was at this very moment galumphing towards a busy main road...

'You left her outside? In this weather?' Striding to the back door, he let out a piercing whistle and a few seconds later the black dog bounded into the kitchen and began to shake itself vigorously.

Cassie backed away to a strategic distance, automatically brushing the spots of muddy water from her skirt.

'Here. Use this.' His movements fluid and economical, Adam Merrick opened the door of the linen cupboard, extracted a towel and tossed it to Cassie.

'Thanks,' she muttered, startled by his consideration, and then as she saw the expression on his face she realised her error. He couldn't be serious, wasn't suggesting that she towel down that monstrous beast. 'I'm not a damn kennel maid.'

'No, you're merely the irresponsible little fool who left Lisa out in the sleet.'

'Oh, for heaven's sake, a few drops of water aren't going to hurt a dog!' The dark, rugged face was as unyielding as rock. Did that hard chiselled mouth ever curve in a smile? Did those chilling eyes ever darken with warmth and humour, crinkle at the corners with laughter?

'Lisa happens to suffer very badly from rheumatism in her hind legs.'

Cassie winced. Thanks, Professor. Make me feel about an inch high. She took a step towards the dog and then halted, irked at the realisation that part of her had acknowledged and was instinctively responding to his indefinable but unmistakable air of authority. Of course she was sorry if she had in any way aggravated Lisa's condition but it had been an honest mistake and she refused to be treated like a recalcitrant child. Make the punishment fit the crime...

She tilted her head upwards and, as the blue eyes drew and held hers, her whole body tensed. This minor confrontation had nothing to do with a wet dog, she registered uneasily, her pulse-rate accelerating. It wasn't even a battle of wills but something far more intangible... Unconsciously her grip on the towel still in her hand tightened, her fingers twining into the deep pile. Dimly she was aware that Lisa had seized the initiative and was rolling herself dry on the hearthrug. Somewhere in the kitchen, a clock ticked away relentlessly.

Abruptly, Adam Merrick turned on his heel. Moving across to a small cabinet high on the wall, he extracted a small bottle, slammed the cabinet closed with a resounding thud, and strode towards the kitchen door.

'Coffee, please. Black. No sugar. Bring it through to my study. First door on the left.'

As his footsteps retreated down the hall, Cassie expelled a long, deep breath, tension easing from her body. What was the matter with her today? she wondered irritably. Allowing a man like Adam Merrick to disturb her, unsettle her by virtue of his physical presence alone? Jet-lag. That was the problem. Her mind and body were still confused, disorientated, making her react and behave uncharacteristically.

'Coffee, please. Black. No sugar.' She mimicked the deep, crisp voice out loud and pulled a face. Oh, what the heck! She was badly in need of coffee herself right now.

She filled up the kettle and, hunting around, discovered the crockery in a clean, orderly cupboard beside the sink unit. It appeared that the chaos was only superficial, doubtless thanks to the efforts of Adam Merrick's efficient housekeeper.

Her eyes alighted on the black dog, flopped out in its basket, and her lips twitched. Mystery of the missing wellies solved. Or at least one of them. That was most definitely a right-footed wellington boot tucked away in the corner of the basket, half hidden under a blanket. A dog with a boot fetish, or was it some sort of security symbol? She shrugged. She wasn't going to waste time trying to psychoanalyse Adam Merrick's dog—although she wouldn't be in the least surprised if it did suffer from severe personality disorders. Living with such a man would drive anyone neurotic...

Some minutes later, armed with a cup of coffee—she'd already gulped down her own reviving brew—Cassie made her way down the hall.

The door of the study was open and for a moment she stood motionless in the doorway, eyes widening incredulously. How could anyone work in this utter confusion of papers and books? They were everywhere, strewn across the large oak table at the far end of the room, stacked in the leather armchair, piled up on the smaller desk around an electric typewriter. Textbooks spilled out of the polished pine bookcase and lined the dark green carpet.

Adam Merrick, apparently oblivious to his surroundings, was sitting behind the oak table, a pile of correspondence in front of him, talking on the telephone extension. Adopting the view that if the call had been private he would have shut the door, Cassie listened unashamedly as she picked her way across the room.

He was, she quickly ascertained, conversing with a local florist, placing an order for a dozen red roses to be sent to Mrs Merrick at an address in Sussex. So Adam Merrick's wife's absence was only temporary... and he was missing her enough to send a floral declaration of his love. Professor Adam Merrick, adoring husband and devoted father... A sudden inexplicable tightness in her chest, Cassie placed the coffee none too gently on his table, spilling some of the contents into the saucer.

'Thank you,' he murmured drily, replacing the receiver. 'Could you open this damn bottle?'

'Child-proof top?' she enquired acidly, taking the bottle of aspirin from his outstretched hand. Deftly removing the top, she handed the bottle back to him, her eyes moving fleetingly over the strong contours of his face. Despite the unruliness of his hair, the stubble on his decisive jaw, this man emitted assurance, competence like a positive charge—and yet he was now apparently defeated by a medicine bottle. Thoughtfully she watched him take out two tablets and swallow them.

'For Pete's sake, woman, don't just stand there. Find a notebook and pencil.'

Cassie's eyes ignited with grey fire. 'Where would you suggest I start looking, Professor Merrick?' she enquired with frigid politeness, deliberately emphasising his name as, raising her eyebrows, she surveyed the chaotic room.

'I can see that the Richardson Agency picks its staff for their initiative as well as their competence,' he answered caustically. 'Try the desk drawer!'

Only one day, Cassie reminded herself as she moved across to the desk. She only had to endure this man for one day. Fishing out a notebook and couple of pencils from the drawer, she spied a hard-backed chair in a corner of the room and walked over to it. Slowly and with great deliberation she picked up the two files on the seat and placed them on the floor.

'Not there, dammit,' he thundered. 'Put them on top of the green file. Beside the cabinet.'

'Yes, Professor,' Cassie murmured innocently. Just as she'd suspected . . . This room might appear to be in a state of complete pandemonium to the uninitiated, but she was willing to bet that Adam Merrick knew exactly where everything was down to the last scrap of paper.

She drew up the chair towards the desk and, turning to a fresh page in her notebook, pencil poised in her hand, looked up at him expectantly. Her shorthand was highly proficient and normally Cassie would have found no difficulty in keeping up with his rapid, fluent dictation but today her fingers seemed uncharacteristically reluctant to obey her commands. Twice she had to ask him to stop and repeat something, bracing herself on each occasion for the expected explosion. But, although the blue eyes reflected his mounting impatience, he made no comment and perversely she found his restraint more unnerving than the anticipated tirade, as if she were waiting for a volcano to erupt.

She was surprised not just by the volume of his correspondence but the variety, having expected it to consist mainly of missives from fellow academics. He courteously refused an invitation to join a panel of literary judges to discuss the merits of various historical novels published during the year, but expressed interest in acting as advisor for a proposed television historical drama series. Cassie guessed from the informality of his reply to the television producer that it was a role he had undertaken before. That he was also much in demand as an after-dinner speaker was another source of surprise. If he accepted even half of the invitations extended to him, he could dine out in style for months, although in fact he declined most of them.

Cassie flexed her aching fingers as he paused to rifle through the pile of letters in front of him. Picking up one, he perused the contents, swivelling sideways in his chair. Casually he crossed one lean leg over the other, the movement causing the denim jeans to tauten across his powerful thighs.

Cassie averted her eyes. Adam Merrick was by no means a handsome man in the classical sense but the harsh, flagrantly male features, the muscular physique, together with the aura of unassailable masculine confidence, were a compelling combination, she admitted with grudging reluctance. He was a man who would always command attention—particularly from gullible women who looked no further than the external trappings of a man, she added acidly. Thank God she could view him with complete detachment, could recognise but remain completely immune to his obvious male attractiveness. There was a tiny nick on his jaw, she noticed absently, as if he'd cut himself starting to shave...

'Would you read that last sentence back to me?'

She jolted, warmth seeping through her body as she stared at the blank page in front of her... Oh, lord, she hadn't even realised he'd resumed his dictation, seemed to have drifted off into a complete daze. 'Um...'

'The Richardson Agency was recommended to me, but I can assure you it isn't a recommendation I shall endorse.' His voice was ominously quiet, almost conversational. 'Miss Richardson evidently doesn't feel the necessity to vet potential staff, simply hires anyone regardless of their competence or experience.'

'I'm perfectly competent,' Cassie shot back, angered more by his criticism of Kate than her own ability. She'd had a couple of lapses in concentration, that's all...not surprising considering she was suffering from jet-lag. 'And I've had dozens of jobs.'

'That doesn't surprise me in the least.'

Cassie's mouth tightened as she heard the derision in his voice, the inference being that she was incapable of obtaining or holding a long-term position.

'Don't just sit there sulking, woman. Before I waste any more of my time, see if you can at least manage to transcribe what you've taken down so far.'

She didn't move. 'Not woman,' she said evenly. The sarcastic, ill-mannered, bad-tempered... 'Cassandra. Cassandra Richardson.' She enunciated her name very slowly and deliberately.

As he raised a dark, quizzical eyebrow at her, she realised how completely ineffectual was her attempt to squash him. He was so thick-skinned, so arrogantly sure of himself, it would probably take a ten-ton truck to do that. Mrs Adam Merrick deserved a medal, suffering this man day after day.

'Richardson,' he murmured thoughtfully. There was a speculative gleam in his eyes that she instantly mistrusted. 'Coincidence, or...?'

'My aunt.'

The blue eyes moved over her set face. 'Oh, I see,' he drawled.

'I doubt it,' Cassie said frigidly, switching on the typewriter. She wasn't going to bite, was going to ignore the obvious insinuation. Was Adam Merrick always so offensive or was there something about her in particular that aroused his antagonism? He'd started sniping at her the minute he'd laid eyes on her... Her eyebrows suddenly furrowed together. Heck, she was slow today. Why hadn't she put two and two together before now? Of course...

Absently she pulled open the desk drawers to look for some typing paper and drew a blank. Her eyes flicked across the room and rested on the dark head bowed over a thick pile of papers. Essays? The first draft of the learned tome? Whatever he was reading, the expression on his face was prohibitive, didn't encourage interruptions. 'Use your initiative, Cassandra,' she muttered sourly and, casting her eyes around the room, discovered a cupboard in the far corner she hadn't noticed before.

Rising to her feet, she walked across to it and on opening the door saw the packs of bond paper on the top shelf. Stretching up on tiptoe, she extracted one.

'And what the hell do you think you're doing?' the deep voice thundered behind her. 'If you wanted some more paper, you could have had the courtesy to ask before you simply started rummaging around.'

She'd had enough! Stormy-eyed, Cassie whirled around to face him. 'Just because your wife's walked out on you and you've a thumping hangover, there's no need to lash out at me! And if you're as big a bastard to live with as work for, I'm not damn well surprised your wife's left you!' She slammed down the paper on the desk. 'And don't bother to fire me, because I quit.'

CHAPTER THREE

ADAM MERRICK threw back his head and roared with laughter.

Stunned into complete silence, Cassie stared at him with disbelief. Whatever response she'd expected, it wasn't this. His teeth gleamed white and even in his dark face, his blue eyes were alive with ill-suppressed amusement, the room resounding with his rich, deep chuckle.

She felt completely deflated, already regretting her outburst, her last vestige of anger now directed inwardly at herself because she'd allowed him to provoke her, needle her into losing her temper. Which made him the victor, not her. And to compound matters, he was actually laughing at her...

'So my wife's abandoned me and I've been drowning my sorrows by hitting the bottle,' he drawled lazily. 'Are you going to tell me how you arrived at this conclusion?'

'The whisky bottle in the kitchen...the black coffee and aspirin,' she muttered stiffly. Only half-aware of what she was doing she returned to the desk and slumped down in her chair. She'd never felt so incredibly foolish in her life. 'And the flowers...'

'Eavesdropping, Miss Richardson, tut, tut.'

'Not having come here equipped with ear-muffs, I could hardly help overhearing,' she flung back. Surely he didn't think she was remotely interested in his personal life?

He leant back in his chair and surveyed her. Surveyed her as if she were a performing animal, Cassie thought savagely, waiting for her to entertain him with her next trick. 'I take it that the roses were a peace offering to

37

my long-suffering wife?' he enquired mockingly. 'A plea for her to return to the marital home?'

She shrugged indifferently. Oh, he was really getting his money's worth out of this one.

'It just happens to be my mother's birthday today,' he continued. His mouth quirked. 'And, contrary to what you might suspect, she also happens to be very happily married to my father.'

Very droll, Cassie thought scathingly, wondering why he was even bothering to offer her an explanation.

'Sorry to disillusion you, but no wife. Not even an estranged one.' Leaning back in his chair he folded his hands behind his head and winced, dropping his right arm back down to the table. As he did so, Cassie caught her first glimpse of the amateurishly applied crêpe bandage beneath the cuff of his sweater. So Professor Merrick had injured himself, had he? Too bad. Although she rather wished she'd known earlier...

'I can also assure you, Miss Richardson, that there is no woman on this earth worth getting drunk over.'

Cassie's head jerked upwards, the sudden harsh cynicism in his voice doubly shocking after the slow, lazy drawl. Her eyes flew to his face but she was too late. Before she'd had a chance to analyse the fleeting expression his eyes, the blue shutters had slammed down, his face a bland, inscrutable mask. Had that simply been his male ego talking or something deeper? She gave a tiny involuntary shudder. He'd sounded so hard...unforgiving...bitter...as if he despised the whole of her sex. Had a woman once actually managed to penetrate that steel armour, inflict a wound that had never healed? Was that why he'd never married? She frowned, a new thought striking her. If he wasn't married... 'William?' she said hesitantly.

'My ward,' he returned casually. Rising to his feet in a swift, controlled movement, he walked over to one of the bookcases and extracted a thick volume with his left hand. 'My brother, William's father, and his wife were

killed in a car crash a year ago,' he continued, returning
to the oak table and placing the book awkwardly in front
of him.

Cassie stiffened, shocked eyes fixed on the dark head,
momentarily repelled by the complete indifference in his
voice and then understanding it. When asked by strangers
about her parents, didn't she too explain that they were
dead in that same cool, expressionless voice?

'I'm sorry,' she muttered inadequately, her eyes dark
with compassion as the image of the small boy she'd
seen earlier swam before her eyes. 'My pa...' she began
shakily, and then snapped her mouth shut. Adam
Merrick wouldn't be interested in her life history. She'd
just wanted to explain that her words of sympathy were
more than simply lip service, that she really understood.
The awful, unbelievable coincidence... Mechanically,
she inserted a sheet of paper into the typewriter and took
a deep breath. Had Adam Merrick taken on the guard-
ianship of his small nephew through choice or had he
simply been motivated by a sense of duty because there
had been no other volunteer?

'Temper tantrum over now? Actually going to settle
down and get on with some work?'

The deep male voice cut across her painful thoughts,
reminded her belatedly that she had theoretically walked
out. 'I'm prepared to give you another chance,' she said
tartly, echoing the words he had spoken to her yesterday.

He regarded her pensively. Why hadn't she been
blessed with eyelashes as thick and dark as those shielding
those disconcerting, vivid blue eyes? Cassie thought in-
consequentially, her heart missing an uncomfortable
beat.

'When you've finished the first letter, perhaps I'd
better check it over before you proceed with the others,
hmm?' he drawled in an aggravatingly calm, patient
voice, the voice of a teacher addressing a pupil who was
experiencing difficulties with its schoolwork.

New tactics, huh? Despite herself, Cassie's lips
twitched. The condescending tolerance in his voice was
far more infuriating than the brusquest of dictatorial
commands, as well he must know. He was also, Cassie
recognised, obliquely reminding her that it was she, as
the mere employee, who was in fact on sufferance. Her
eyes dropped from his face and encountered the
sprinkling of fine dark hairs at the V of his cashmere
jumper, and whatever response she'd been intending to
make died in her throat.

Bowing her head over the typewriter, shielding her face
from the discerning blue eyes, her fingers began to move
swiftly over the keyboard. Completing the letter in record
time, she scanned it quickly for errors and then, sat-
isfied, removed it from the typewriter. She rose to her
feet and, moving across to the oak table, placed the letter
wordlessly in front of him. If Adam Merrick wanted to
waste time playing juvenile games, who cared? The
agency was charging him by the hour. Hell, she felt like
a school-girl waiting to have her homework marked...

He ran his eye swiftly over the letter and looked up
at her. 'Well done, Cassandra,' he murmured
approvingly.

Cassie smiled back, her fingernails digging painfully
into the palm of her clenched fist. Oh, go boil your head
in oil, Professor.

Automatically picking up a pen to sign the letter, he
muttered a mild curse and the pen fell from his right
hand.

'Painful, hmm?' Cassie murmured with wide, innocent
grey eyes. Agony probably, she thought cheerfully,
turning away.

'Doesn't your aunt pay you enough to buy a pair of
shoes?'

She paused, startled, and looked down at her stock-
inged feet. It was oddly disconcerting to know that he
had been watching her walk back across the room. She'd

discarded her hated shoes under the desk, she remembered now. 'Bunions,' she said airily.

'Must be very painful,' he murmured sympathetically. 'You ought to see a chiropodist,' he added solicitously.

'And you should see a doctor, Professor Merrick,' she returned sweetly, echoing the exaggerated concern in his own voice. 'Have your wrist X-rayed. Even if it's only sprained, the hospital might give you some painkillers.' Which hopefully might knock you out cold for the rest of the day.

The blue shutters slammed down over his eyes. 'When I want your advice, Miss Richardson, I shall ask for it,' he said curtly. 'And I should like those letters completed before the end of the day, if you can possibly manage that,' he added with heavy sarcasm.

Her face tightening, Cassie whipped round, stalked over to her desk and inserted a sheet of paper none too gently into the typewriter. There had been absolutely no need to snap her head off like that. Her fingers began to pound across the keyboard and then she stopped, taking a deep breath. Calm down, Cassandra, before you use up the entire spool of correction tape. Just concentrate on what you're doing. Block that obnoxious man sitting on the other side of the room right out of your mind. Don't even glance at him.

As she completed the last letter, she finally lifted her head and was disconcerted to find the blue eyes focused on her face. To her intense irritation she found herself flushing slightly under his pensive gaze. How long had he been sitting there watching her? Or was it simply that she was in his line of vision? She looked back at him with a blank, expressionless face.

'Have you ever shaved a man?'

'What?' She was thrown completely off balance. Of course she'd never shaved a man. What a damn fool question. 'Only with cut-throat razors,' she said acidly. She didn't trust that glint in his eyes, nor the con-

templative way he was rubbing his darkened jaw with
his left hand. 'I'm not——'

'Yes, I know,' he cut in drily. 'You're not a damn
barber.'

'You don't want a secretary, you want a slave!' So she
was predictable now, was she? Add it to the list: irresponsible, aggressive, incompetent—and unfeminine. She
must remind herself to ask him for a character reference
before she left! It was infuriating to realise that it was
the charge of being unfeminine that most rankled. 'Or
a submissive little wifey to run around after you,' she
added bitingly.

'Now that sounds an excellent idea,' he mused, raising
a thoughtful dark eyebrow. 'Although it's hardly a role
I can see you in.'

'I wasn't applying,' she said tartly. For either role!

The straight mouth suddenly quirked, the blue eyes
darkening until they were almost navy. The smile trans-
formed his face, softened the harsh male features, and
Cassie's heart skipped an involuntary beat.

'I know it's not part of your job description or the
most usual of requests, but I would be grateful,' he said
quietly. 'This damn stubble itches like hell.'

If he thought she was going to go weak at the knees,
be swayed by a pair of deep blue eyes and a persuasive
voice, he was a hundred per cent wrong. He was in-
credible! He'd been rude and abrasive most of the
morning and he thought that all he had to do was smile
and she would melt into a lump of malleable putty,
acquiesce to his every wish.

The sleet had stopped and the rays from a watery sun
suddenly filled the room, touched the dark head, igniting it with blue-black flames. Cassie swallowed, trying
to moisten the sudden dryness in her throat. What would
it feel like to curl her hands through the thick richness
of his hair, to trace the contours of the square, strong
jawline, not with a razor, but with her fingertips? She
flinched, her eyes widening with alarm, appalled at her

line of thought, a pulse beginning to beat erratically at the base of her neck.

'For Pete's sake, don't look so damned terrified!' Adam Merrick's voice cracked through the air like a whip. Kicking back his chair, he rose to his feet and crossed the carpet with swift, jerky strides. 'I'm asking you to shave me, not go to bed with me!'

'Don't be so ridiculous!' Cassie glared up at the figure looming over her.

'I can assure you I'm not in the habit of seducing my secretaries,' he continued icily, ignoring her interruption. Slowly and deliberately his gaze dropped from her face and moved insolently over the slender curves of her body. 'And I hardly think you're going to be the exception to the rule,' he finished contemptuously.

'I can assure you I wouldn't want to be!' she bit back, her eyes narrowed. What would it be like to be seduced by this man? To be coaxed by his mouth, his voice, his hands into total submission? She recoiled as the unwanted thought crept insidiously into her mind, rejecting it furiously. 'All right,' she heard a voice bellow, and with shock realised that it was her own. 'Go and fetch your lousy razor.'

He smiled. 'As you wish,' he murmured with aggravating courtesy, sauntering casually towards the door. 'I'll bring it down to the kitchen.'

As he disappeared into the hall, Cassie slammed her small fist down in front of her, letting out a yelp of pain as her knuckles hit the edge of the desk. That smug, complacent expression on his arrogant face as he'd left the room! He was so damn sure of himself, so confident of always getting his own way. She felt as if she'd been manipulated, pushed into a corner. Her mouth tightened. Just because she hadn't jumped to obey his royal command—ill-disguised as a request—he'd made her sound like a nervous teenager, scared to death of coming within arm's reach of a man in case he turned into a raving sex maniac. A small, unwilling grin touched her lips. Well, her experience of men was limited—but that was through choice not because of any hang-up! Her nomadic existence precluded long-term relationships and she wasn't interested in having a succession of brief, casual affairs. Maybe she was old-fashioned but she'd decided in her late teens that, for her, sex would have to be synonymous with love, an emotional as well as physical union. If she ever did make that final commitment it would have to be to a man she loved, respected . . . and trusted.

'Are you sure you know what you're doing, Kate? Exactly what you're taking on? Cassie isn't an easy child to love. I know it's not her fault but if only she weren't such a quiet, plain, skinny . . .'

Cassie's eyes darkened. Why did those words still come back to haunt her after all these years? And what had forced them out of her subconscious at this precise moment, for Pete's sake? She shrugged dismissively. The past couldn't wound her any more. She was a secure, confident adult now, she reminded herself firmly. Those childhood scars had long since healed.

'Cassandra!' The deep, commanding male voice echoed resoundingly down the hall.

'Coming, lord and master,' she muttered acidly, touching an imaginary forelock. She pushed back her chair and made her way unhurriedly across the room and down the hall to the kitchen.

Her features schooled into an expression of acute boredom, she paused in the open doorway and watched as Adam Merrick, a towel flung across his broad shoulders, left-handedly covered the lower half of his face with shaving soap. She'd never actually witnessed a man shaving before, she thought uneasily, hadn't realised until now how oddly disturbing was the wholly masculine activity, even the preliminaries.

Turning away from the sink unit, he drew up a kitchen stool and sat down, stretching out his long lean legs indolently in front of him.

'Ready?' he drawled, lifting a dark eyebrow at her.

She shrugged nonchalantly and, moving across to the kitchen table, picked up the razor. She was puzzled by his rapid mood change and, instead of welcoming it, found his air of relaxed good humour profoundly irritating, contrasting as it did right now so markedly with her own ebbing confidence. She bent her head towards his face and brushed an ineffectual, tentative sweep across his chin with the razor.

'I'm not made of glass,' he said drily.

No, she thought with ferocious resentment, he was made of hard sinews and solid muscle, a warm, breathing male animal.

'And it might help if you held my head.'

Cassie gave another careless shrug, avoiding his eyes. Imagine you're a hairdresser, a nurse, a dentist. View the man sitting on that stool with complete impersonal detachment. Oh, hell... Gritting her teeth, she placed her hand on the side of his head, instantly conscious of the dark hair springing beneath her palm. Concentrate, Cassandra, concentrate. Her fingers tightened around the razor.

'Ouch!'

'It's only a tiny nick! And if you'd just keep still...'

The stubble began to disappear beneath her hand, the strong planes of his face becoming more defined. There was a cleft in the square, tenacious chin she hadn't noticed before... nor had she realised just how sensuous was the curve of his lower lip...

'For Pete's sake...'

'I told you to keep still!' She tossed the razor into the sink. 'That's it. I've finished.' Turning around, she tripped over his outstretched legs and fell headlong towards him.

As she instinctively grasped hold of his shoulders to try and steady herself, she heard his sharp intake of breath, saw a reflection of her own shock in the shadowy depths of his eyes.

The firm, straight mouth was on a level with her own, only inches away, and she could feel the warmth of his breath on her face. She was appallingly aware that her breasts were pressed against the hard wall of his chest, that her legs were resting with terrifying intimacy between two muscular thighs. The blood pounded in her ears, warmth scorching through her veins. For a second she was incapable of coherent thought, let alone moving, had never felt so vulnerable, so defenceless in her entire adult life, powerless to protect herself against the unwanted, alien sensations taunting every nerve-ending in her body. Then something inside her head exploded.

Pushing roughly against the powerful shoulders, she scrambled upright.

'I could have broken my neck falling over your damn feet.'

He lifted a dark eyebrow. 'Don't you think you're over-reacting somewhat?' he drawled.

Lips compressed disdainfully together, Cassie's gaze didn't waver from the dark, mocking face. She'd completely betrayed herself by that burst of anger, she realised, squirming inwardly. He was so arrogantly sure of himself, she thought savagely, so convinced that no woman could come within his sphere and remain immune to his blatant, raw masculinity—and her wilful, traitorous hormones had played right into his egoistical hands.

'Just be grateful I shan't be pressing charges.'

'What?' Cassie's eyes narrowed as she watched him rise leisurely to his feet.

'Sexual harassment. Isn't that what you'd be screaming if the roles had been reversed and I'd lunged towards you?'

'You're crazy...I tripped over your feet...You don't think I deliberately...' Cassie saw the glint in his eyes. He was deliberately winding her up, amused by her flustered, vehement protests. The corners of the straight mouth quirked and some part of her almost responded,

visualising just how absurd she must look, standing there
glowering up at him, cheeks flushed, bristling with indignation. But she ruthlessly quelled the bubble of
laughter rising in her throat. She didn't want to share
anything with this man, certainly not laughter.

She frowned, watching him from under her eyelashes
as he picked up the waxed jacket from the chair where
he'd discarded it earlier.

'Go and fetch your coat, Cassandra,' he murmured
over his shoulder.

She didn't move. 'We're going on an outing?' she enquired sweetly.

'Hospital.'

Cassie's eyes sparked. 'What period of history do you
teach, Professor Merrick? The Dark Ages? Contrary to
what you obviously believe, the word "secretary" is no
longer a euphemism for general dogsbody and coffee-
making machine.' Of course she didn't mind taking him
to the hospital—but he could ask, not simply bark out
an order as if she were his flipping dog?

'Quite finished?' he enquired mildly.

Oh, what was the use? Cassie stomped across the
kitchen into the hall. It was like trying to talk to a brick
wall. She lifted her duffel coat off the peg and shrugged
it on. The best solution was to simply ignore Adam
Merrick from now on, not to react to anything he said
or did, she decided resolutely.

The only problem was, she decided uneasily some five
minutes later as she guided Kate's car down the lane,
that he was not the easiest of men to ignore. She couldn't
relax, was acutely conscious of the dominant male
presence beside her in the passenger seat.

As she paused at a junction, she flicked him a surreptitious glance from under her thick lashes, her eyes
moving swiftly over the strong, rugged features. It
wouldn't kill him to make some attempt at conversation, pass the odd comment, just to show he was aware

that there was another human being in the car with him. He hadn't spoken one word since they'd left the cottage.

'Lights have turned green,' the deep voice suddenly murmured helpfully.

'I'm perfectly aware of that,' Cassie said haughtily, her eyes darting back to the road. She pressed her foot on the accelerator and the car stalled. Humming nonchalantly under her breath, she turned on the ignition and moved forward.

'Have you any plans for tonight, Cassandra?'

Having mentally steeled herself to counteract some caustic comment about female drivers, she was completely taken aback by the unexpected question. Instinctively her eyes slid to his face but she could learn nothing from his bland expression. Had any other man posed that question, she would have suspected that he was about to follow it up with an invitation... Her stomach muscles clenched. Surely Adam Merrick wouldn't have the audacity, the utter gall, to think that she would willingly spend a moment longer in his obnoxious company than was necessary. Surely even he couldn't be that thick-skinned...

'Nothing special,' she finally answered casually, and out of the corner of her eye saw his brief smile of satisfaction. Her own lips curved as she anticipated his next words. Oh, she was going to savour this moment, relish pricking that over-inflated male ego...

'Good,' he drawled. 'While I'm at the hospital, perhaps you'd like to go home and pack an overnight case.'

'An overnight case?' Cassie echoed.

'I'm a little possessive about my toothbrush and presumably you'd like a change of clothes for the morning.'

She wasn't hearing this, Cassie thought incredulously. Adam Merrick was calmly and blatantly proposing she spend the night with him! It wouldn't be the first time a male employer had evinced more than a purely professional interest in her, but at least they had made some attempt at subtlety.

She wanted to laugh in his face, but her throat constricted and the sound wouldn't come. With disturbing clarity she recalled the moment she'd fallen headlong against him in the kitchen, could almost feel the pressure of the powerful male body against hers, smell the clean, soapy scent of his skin. Adam Merrick was too experienced, too astute a man not to have been fully aware of her reaction to him and, because of that second's aberration on her part, now apparently assumed that she would be more than willing to share his bed. The car came to a shuddering halt as she slammed on the brakes. 'You must be joking!' Her eyes blazed into his. 'If you think I'd...'

'A simple no would have sufficed,' he murmured mildly. 'I merely thought you might be interested in earning a little extra cash.'

'You were going to pay me?'

'Well, naturally.' He looked surprised. 'I'd hardly expect you to mind William as a favour,' he added drily.

'You want me to babysit for William?' Oh, God, please find me a big deep hole to crawl in. How could she have been such a stupid little fool? The car moved forward. What was it about this man that seemed to make her take leave of all rationality and common sense, reduce her to the level of an hysterical adolescent?

'I've a dinner engagement tonight. Mrs Evans was going to mind William but that's obviously now out of the question. As I shall probably be home very late, I thought it would be more convenient for you to stay the night.' The blue eyes explored her face. 'What exactly did you think I was suggesting?' he enquired casually.

Cassie shrugged, keeping her eyes fixed steadily on the road in front, but the betraying colour crept up her neck, burnt into her face.

'Ah, I see,' the deep voice mused pensively. 'Your fertile little imagination has been in overdrive again.

After an acquaintance of a few hours, you thought I was inviting you to spend a night of unbridled passion with me, hmm?' The blue eyes glinted, raking her crimson face unmercifully. 'I'm curious. Was I going to wine and dine you first or were we going to dispense with all the time-wasting preliminaries?' He paused. 'Ever considered professional help? You obviously have some deep-rooted problem if you think every man you meet is hell-bent on luring you into his bed.' Abruptly he threw back his head and burst into laughter. 'And you actually thought I was going to pay for the privilege...'

Cassie's hands tightened around the steering-wheel until her knuckles whitened as the mocking laughter reverberated around the car once again, wondering if she had ever loathed another human being quite so much in her entire life. It was all sheer guesswork on his part. He couldn't possibly know for certain just how accurate was his synopsis of her thoughts. Keep cool. Don't over-react. She reduced speed as they reached the outskirts of the town. If he'd wanted her to babysit for William, why couldn't he have simply said so straight out at the beginning instead of being so ambiguous? she thought with searing resentment. The realisation hit her like a hammer. He'd been evasive on purpose, had been winding her up all along, playing an infantile game with her for his own perverse amusement. He'd deliberately set out to make a fool of her.

'No. You managed that quite successfully on your own.'

She stiffened. How had he known...?

'You shouldn't jump to conclusions, make snap judgements,' he continued quietly. 'It's a dangerous game.'

Cassie's jaw tightened. Who the hell did he think he was? The sanctimonious, patronising prig. Swinging right, she drove through the hospital entrance and pulled up into a parking space. She kept her eyes focused directly ahead as she heard the click of the seatbelt and the door opening.

'Pick me up at twelve.'

Teeth clenched together, she nodded. For a supposedly articulate man, he had an extremely limited vocabulary, had evidently never heard of the simple word please.

'That should give you time to collect your overnight things.'

Cassie jerked her head towards him. The man had a skin like a rhinoceros! 'I've already told you——'

'I'll pay double the going rate.'

She took a quick controlling breath. 'I suppose it hadn't occurred to you simply to cancel your dinner engagement?' she enquired icily.

'It would be extremely inconvenient to do so.'

'Inconvenient?' she repeated slowly. 'Is that how you regard William too? As an inconvenience? An unwanted intrusion into your bachelor life...' She snapped her mouth shut, could have bitten off her tongue, regretted the cheap jibe the moment the words left her lips. What the hell had possessed her to make such an unfounded accusation? But it was too late...

A muscle flickered along the line of the hard jaw. 'Abandoned husband, sex maniac, and now wicked uncle.' Adam Merrick's voice was quiet, controlled, but the contempt in his eyes made her flinch. 'My God, what a nauseating, sordid, petty little mind you have, Miss Richardson.' Turning abruptly on his heel, he strode across the car park, leaving Cassie staring after his tall retreating figure with large, unhappy eyes.

Clasping a small canvas bag in her hand, Cassie descended the stairs from the flat, gave a perfunctory knock on Kate's office door and walked in.

'You've changed,' her aunt observed.

'Mmm. More practical for small boys and shaggy dogs,' Cassie murmured, glancing down at her jeans and blue sweatshirt.

'So what's he like?' Kate put down her pen and smiled over the desk top.

'Fine. No problem. The perfect employer,' Cassie returned cheerfully, pulling up a chair.

Kate grinned. 'That bad, huh?'

'Worse.'

'And yet you're going to babysit for his nephew tonight?' Kate murmured, her dark eyes thoughtful as they rested on her niece's oddly subdued face.

Cassie's eyes dropped to the carpet. 'A bit of extra cash is always useful, especially with Christmas coming up.' She knew she hadn't fooled Kate for a second, but wasn't sure herself why she'd changed her mind. It wasn't if she really cared a hoot what Adam Merrick thought of her, or was trying to make amends...

As Kate stretched out a hand to answer the telephone, Cassie rose to her feet. 'Coffee?' she mouthed, and disappeared into the tiny kitchenette concealed behind a sliding door at one end of the office. Who was Adam Merrick dining with tonight? That he had a woman, or even several, in his life she didn't doubt for second. What sort of woman would appeal to him? She shook her head irritably. She wasn't even remotely interested in Adam Merrick's love-life.

'That was Richard,' her aunt said casually as Cassie returned with two mugs and a plate of digestive biscuits. 'He's invited me to a charity dinner at Tanworth Hall tonight. His mother's one of the organisers. Heaven knows what I'm going to wear.'

'You always look terrific in that black dress.' Cassie helped herself to a biscuit and then frowned. 'Richard called just now... to invite you out this evening? Oh, Kate, you didn't say that you'd go?'

'I'm not a fool,' Kate said drily. 'Whoever Richard was originally taking to the dinner has obviously cried off at the last minute. Probably gone down with this flu bug.'

'But you're still going to go?'

'Cass, would you stop looking at me like that? Richard and I are just friends, that's all.' Kate shrugged. 'It's no big deal.'

Cassie glared down at her mug of coffee. Why couldn't Richard see how much he kept hurting Kate? And why did Kate allow him to treat her like this? She was an attractive, intelligent, successful woman. Hardly doormat material. Which made it all the more baffling that she allowed Richard to trample over her feelings time after time. The most frustrating thing of all was that she was convinced that Richard reciprocated Kate's feelings—he just needed some sort of sharp shock to make him come to his senses. Like the sudden realisation that he was in danger of losing Kate to another man. Nothing like a bit of good healthy jealousy. She grinned inwardly, mocking herself. Of course she was the world's expert on relationships. She drained her coffee-mug and flicked a glance at the wall clock.

'Better be off,' she murmured. 'And have a super time tonight.'

She saw him the moment she walked into the hospital entrance, sitting in a hard chair in the reception area, one long, lean leg crossed over the other, reading a newspaper. Unconsciously she paused, her eyes drawn like a magnet to the strong, assured face, absorbing every detail of the aggressively male features. He wasn't a handsome man in the strictest sense of the word, his features were too individual for that, but she admitted with an uneasy thump of her heart that he was undoubtedly the most compelling man she had ever seen in her life.

Hesitantly she moved towards him. 'Ready?' Her voice was unnaturally brusque, her eyes wary.

His expression was bland as he lifted his head from the paper and rose lazily to his feet. 'Bang on time,' he murmured approvingly, glancing up at the wall clock. 'Good girl.'

'Do I get rewarded with walkies later?' Cassie enquired sarcastically as they emerged into the open air and walked across the car park. She began to relax, relieved but puzzled that he seemed to have completely forgotten the tension under which they'd parted. 'Or a nice juicy marrowbone?' She fished out the car keys from her pocket and unlocked the car door.

The straight mouth quirked. 'I was rather thinking along the lines of a ploughman's. I could murder a pint.' He folded his long, powerful frame into the passenger seat beside her. 'We'll stop off at the Old Oaks on the way back.'

'Oh, goody,' Cassie muttered under her breath. A treat for the little minion from the feudal lord. She saw his eyes flicker to the canvas bag on the rear seat.

'I——'

'Yes, I know,' he cut in drily. 'You're not doing it to help me out but because you feel sorry for William.'

Mechanically, Cassie switched on the engine, turning left out of the hospital to join the steady stream of traffic heading away from the town. 'Look, I'm...sorry. I shouldn't have said...' She paused, waiting for him to say something, but he remained completely silent. Her hackles rose. She'd been adult enough to swallow her pride and apologise and it wouldn't hurt him to do likewise. She turned off the main road into a country lane. Heck, she wished she hadn't bothered to say anything now.

'So what's the verdict on the wrist?' she asked cheerfully. It was impossible to tell under the jacket whether it was in plaster or not. 'Broken?' she added hopefully.

'Sprained. Just as I suspected.'

Of course he would be right. 'I expect it's still very painful,' she murmured sweetly, swinging the car into the gravel sweep outside an old half-timbered inn. She felt his eyes exploring her face as the car came to a halt.

'Charitable little thing, aren't you?' he observed quietly.

She didn't answer, oddly disconcerted by the remark, and, releasing her seatbelt, clambered swiftly from the car.

The lounge bar of the popular country inn was crowded when they walked in, but Adam Merrick's height and breadth made an immediate path for them as they approached the bar.

'What would you like to drink?' He tilted his head towards Cassie.

'White wine, please.' She was irked to notice just how quickly he'd commanded the attention of the attractive barmaid and wondered wryly if she would have received such instant service had she been on her own.

Her gaze wandered around the room. The log fire blazing in the large open fireplace, the Christmas decorations adorning the smoke-blackened beams, generated a festive air. Idly Cassie watched an earnest, bespectacled girl, a university scarf draped around her neck, detach herself from a group near the fire and edge her way towards the bar.

'Why don't you go and grab a table?'

Cassie nodded and picked up her glass. Turning away, she collided with the approaching girl.

'Sorry,' Cassie murmured automatically.

The girl, her intense gaze focused on the tall, lean dark-haired man at the bar, ignored her completely.

'Professor Merrick...I'm sorry to interrupt you...but I was wondering ... I'm having the most terrible trouble with that assignment and...'

Cassie began to move away. The girl was evidently one of his students and, judging from her tense expression and breathless rush of disjointed words, a very agitated one.

'We'll discuss it next term.'

Startled by the harshness in the deep voice, Cassie flicked a glance back over her shoulder and was shocked to see the ice in the blue eyes, the forbidding line of the firm mouth. For Pete's sake, the poor girl had only been asking for some help, some reassurance with her studies. Maybe it was the vacation, but even so...

She spotted an empty table near the door and slipped into a chair. Taking a sip from her glass, she watched Adam Merrick cross the lounge towards her, observing with suppressed irritation the number of female heads that turned in his direction. Was he aware of the attention he was attracting or was he so accustomed to drawing female eyes that it no longer even registered with him? No wonder he was so appallingly arrogant...

'I've ordered a ploughman's each,' he announced as he joined her.

'Thanks.' It gave her a perverse satisfaction to see how uncomfortable he looked cramping his muscular length into the restricted space opposite her.

He took a long draught of beer and surveyed her over the rim of his glass. 'So how long have you been working for your aunt's agency, Cassandra?' he asked idly.

She shrugged. 'I don't. At least not on a permanent basis. Just occasionally when I'm home.' As he raised a quizzical eyebrow, she added reluctantly, 'I've been in Australia for the last ten months.'

'Hence the profusion of tiny freckles on your nose,' he murmured, and smiled. 'Or are they a permanent fixture, summer and winter?'

'Afraid so,' she said lightly. She was startled by his observation, startled too to realise that she had the most burning desire to know whether he happened to like freckles. She leant back in her chair and took another long sip of wine.

Whether it was the effect of the wine or the festive atmosphere of the pub she wasn't sure, but she began to relax, feeling more at ease than she had all morning and, by the time the waitress appeared with their lunch order, was secretly amazed to discover that she was actually enjoying Adam Merrick's company.

He was a skilled, well informed, amusing raconteur and she began to appreciate why he was in such demand as an after-dinner speaker. And, much to her intense surprise, he also proved to be an excellent listener. Under his gentle prompting, she talked about her travels, discovering from his reaction to some of her own anecdotes that he shared her slightly off-beat sense of humour.

'And you stay with your aunt between trips?'

Cassie swallowed a mouthful of crusty bread and cheese. It was impossible to believe that the man sitting opposite her, an expression of genuine interest in the dark blue eyes, was the one she'd first encountered this morning. 'My parents were killed when I was nine,' she explained in an unemotional, matter-of-fact voice. 'Kate, my aunt, brought me up.'

'She's your only relative?'

'No, she just happened to win the toss,' Cassie returned flippantly. Unable to hold his gaze, her eyes dropped, encompassing the strong lean hands resting palms down on the table opposite her. Long, supple fingers, short, surgically clean nails. Capable yet oddly sensitive hands. They looked as if they would always smell of soap, be oddly reassuring to touch, to hold. For Pete's sake, Cassandra! She took a swift gulp from her glass.

'How long do you intend to stay in England this time?'

She glanced up and shrugged. 'I'm not sure,' she admitted honestly. Each time she returned, she genuinely intended to settle down, but then that restlessness would start... 'Have backpack, will travel,' she murmured with a grin, the grin faltering as she encountered his stony gaze, thrown completely off balance by his abrupt mood change.

'And is that how you plan to spend the rest of your life? Living out of a rucksack? Avoiding all responsibility, commitment?' The contempt in his voice was mirrored in the dark blue depths of his eyes, etched into every harsh line of his granite face.

Cassie stiffened. Who the hell did he think he was, condemning her...? He was making her sound like some feckless, immature teenager. A few brief moments ago, she'd actually wondered if she'd misjudged this man, had actually thought she could grow to like him... 'Lots of people take some time off before settling down.' She was irritated to hear how defensive she sounded.

He lifted a dark eyebrow. 'Four years?' he enquired sardonically.

Cassie lifted her chin. She wasn't going to be browbeaten, wasn't going to apologise for the way she chose to live her own life. 'I happen to enjoy——'

'Living from day to day?' he cut in. 'A succession of casual temporary jobs.' His voice hardened. 'And a succession of equally casual temporary relationships, hmm?'

CHAPTER FOUR

SHE wasn't hearing this, Cassie thought incredulously, the disgust in the harsh voice leaving her in no doubt as to the implication of his last words. Casual temporary relationships... He meant affairs, a string of lovers, was virtually accusing her of having slept her way as well as having worked her way around the world. Her stomach knotted with revulsion, anger tearing through her.

'I hardly think that my personal life is any of your damn business, Professor Merrick!' Her carefree, no-madic existence must automatically indicate an equally carefree, casual attitude to sex. Is that how his contemptible, bigoted, shallow little mind worked? She suddenly felt completely cold, icily calm. Slowly and deliberately she picked up her wine.

'Tsk, tsk. Temper, temper!' drawled the deep voice. But Cassie barely registered the words, aware only of the strong lean fingers closing over hers as he pried the glass from her unresisting grasp, the warmth from his hand scalding up her arm. Her heart hammered in her chest, pumping the heated blood through her veins to every nerve-ending in her body. She detested this man, despised him, and yet his slightest casual touch could send these shock-waves coursing through her, she thought with appalled disbelief. How could her mind and body be so out of tune? How could she feel even the slightest spark of physical attraction for a man who repelled her mentally?

She felt his eyes on her averted face, drawing her own like a magnet, compelling her against her will to look up at him. Slowly she raised her head and cringed inwardly as she read the humiliating message in the taunting, mocking blue depths that told her more ex-

plicitly than any words that he was aware of the reason
for the agitation in her eyes, the flush in her cheeks.
Aware and arrogantly amused. He was a man who would
enjoy exerting his sexual power over women, she thought
with loathing, would enjoy seeing how quickly he could
mould them into submissive, mindless lumps of putty
beneath his experienced hands. And then doubtless despise them afterwards for acquiescing too easily,
condemn them just as he had unjustifiably condemned
her.

'Professor Merrick?'

As if from a great distance Cassie heard the alien voice
and, jerking her head around, saw the student who had
approached Adam Merrick earlier standing by their table.
Her eyes were focused intently on the seated man.

'I was—um, wondering if I could buy you a drink...
I mean it's nearly Christmas...'

'We were just leaving.'

Cassie barely had time to register the cold, brusque
dismissal, the look of mortification on the girl's scarlet
face, before she found herself being unceremoniously
yanked to her feet and propelled towards the door.

'You ill-mannered oaf!' Cassie threw off the restraining hand on her arm the second they emerged into
the cold air, her eyes sparking with furious grey fire.
How dared he damn well march her out of the pub as
if she'd been a recalcitrant child?

He ignored her completely, striding across the car park,
almost forcing her to jog-trot to keep up.

'You're the most cold-blooded, inhuman, insensitive... That poor girl was one of your students and
you treated her as if she's just crawled out of a hole.'
Her voice rose as she glowered up at the shuttered, expressionless face. 'You humiliated her! But then that's
your speciality, isn't it, Professor Merrick, humiliating
women?' Infuriated by his continuing lack of reaction,
she changed tack. 'What's the matter with her? Isn't she

attractive enough to warrant a few seconds of your time?'
she jeered.

As he ground to an abrupt halt, a muscle flickering
along the line of the hard jaw, Cassie felt a wave of vic-
torious satisfaction that she had finally succeeded in
provoking him. She squared her small chin, adrenalin
surging through her as she waited for the anticipated explosion. Go on. Fire me. Terminate my employment as
from now. She lifted her eyes challengingly to his face
and faltered, deflation pricking her as she encountered
his bland expression.

'Of course. How crass of me not to have realised,' the
deep voice drawled conversationally. The firm mouth
quirked into an understanding, sympathetic smile.
'Hormonal, hmm?'

'What?' For a second Cassie wondered if she'd heard
correctly. Hormonal! 'Of all the patronising, condescending, sexist, chauvinistic——'

'That's right. Let it all out of your system,' he cut in
smoothly as she gulped for breath. The blue eyes reflected the tolerant, slightly bored patience of an adult
humouring a child in a temper tantrum. 'Have a good
scream. Stamp your feet.'

'Go to hell!'

The deep mocking laugh followed her as Cassie swung
away and stalked across to the car. He'd won again,
hands down, she thought savagely, clenching her teeth
together. Any decent self-respecting boss would have
fired her for her outburst—justified though it had been.
But she hadn't even managed to ruffle Adam Merrick's
iron composure, let alone goad him into losing his
temper, she thought furiously. In fact she doubted
whether anything she'd said had even penetrated that
arrogant, egoistical dark head. She fumbled in her pocket
for the car keys and unlocked the door. For two pins,
she'd drive away and leave him stranded. He could get
a taxi, hitch a lift, walk...

Slipping into the driver's seat, she took a long, deep breath. Why did she allow him to keep winding her up like this? Why didn't she simply treat him with the cold disdain he deserved? After all she wasn't being paid to like him, merely to carry out her requisite duties as efficiently as possible. His personality defects were none of her concern.

Turning her head, she watched him approach the car, his long, fluid strides already disquietingly familiar, and without warning her stomach dipped. Swiftly she averted her gaze, tensing as he opened the door and folded his muscular length into the seat beside her.

The second she heard the click of his seatbelt, she started up the engine, drove across the car park and then, disconcerted by his continuing silence, she flicked him a quick exploratory glance. He seemed to have forgotten her existence completely, was leaning back against the head-rest, blue eyes dark and shuttered, lost in his own private world. Well, at least she wouldn't be subject to any more of his puerile comments. She scowled as she swung out into the lane, infuriated to realise that some perverse feminine part of her resented that he had dismissed her so easily from his mind, resented even more the fact that she was unable to emulate him. She was driving on auto-pilot, all her senses dominated by the masculine presence beside her, alert to his slightest movement. Her eyes slid to his face, moved over the tenacious jaw, dropped to the firm, straight mouth and decisive, square chin. She yanked her eyes back to the narrow, winding lane. If she didn't start concentrating they were going to end up in the ditch...

The moment she drew up in front of the red-brick cottage, she reached for the door-handle and scrambled out, relief flooding her as she escaped the claustrophobic confines of the car. She slammed the door shut and her eyes alighted briefly on the canvas hold-all lying on the back seat. Huh. Turning away, she followed the retreating figure around the side of the cottage. Adam Merrick could whistle for a babysitter tonight!

Lisa greeted her master rapturously as he opened the back door, gave Cassie a disdainful sniff and padded back to her basket. Which just went to prove how wrong was the old adage about animals and children, Cassie mused acidly. There were two wellington boots tucked into the basket now. Doubly insecure when the master was away? she wondered absently as she registered the immaculate state of the kitchen.

As if on cue the hall door opened and a diminutive grey-haired woman, in the process of fastening the buttons of a fawn raincoat, bustled into the kitchen.

'You must be Emily.' Adam Merrick advanced towards her with a smile, hand outstretched.

To Cassie's intense satisfaction, she ignored both his hand and smile. 'Mrs Thomas,' she corrected him severely, and moved purposefully across to the windowsill on which were displayed the razor and shaving cream. 'The kitchen is no place for this sort of thing.' She held the offending articles aloft as if they were the chief exhibit in a court case, brown button eyes radiating intense disapproval. 'And I discovered——' she paused '—a bone under the table.' She looked up accusingly at the towering, dark-haired man as if he were personally responsible for the heinous crime. 'It has now been disposed of.'

Cassie bit her lip as she saw the bemused expression on the strong, rugged face. Any minute now the tiny little woman was going to demand to know if he'd wiped his feet, she thought, fighting back the bubbles of laughter in her throat. It was like watching a man-eating tiger being mesmerised by a mouse.

'There's a casserole in the oven,' Mrs Thomas continued, moving towards the door. She turned on the threshold. 'I can give you two hours tomorrow,' she announced with largesse, sniffed and disappeared.

There was a moment's silence as the door closed behind her.

'She—um—seems very efficient,' Cassie murmured gravely, swallowing hard.

'Extremely competent,' Adam Merrick agreed with equal gravity. The straight mouth began to quirk and as Cassie's eyes met and locked into the blue ones, she lost the battle and dissolved into laughter, tension easing from her body.

'Actually I rather liked her,' she confessed weakly as she sobered up. If only for the fact that the other woman had been completely unintimidated by Adam Merrick, she decided, surveying him across the kitchen.

'We had a cook very much like her when I was a child,' he drawled unexpectedly, removing his jacket and tossing it carelessly over a chair. 'She used to terrorise the rest of the staff and yet they all secretly adored her.' He smiled reflectively as he strode to the door. 'Whenever my parents had a dinner party, she used to smuggle titbits upstairs for me.'

So even as a small boy Adam Merrick had apparently had women eating out of his hand, Cassie mused acidly as she followed him into the hall, intrigued despite herself by the small insight into his background, a background that had evidently been an affluent one. Well, not this woman! Laughter might have released her anger, but had done nothing to dissipate her antipathy towards him, she reminded herself determinedly as she hung up her coat and entered the study, and then wondered a little uneasily why it seemed so necessary to re-endorse that fact.

She sat down behind her desk and, correctly anticipating that he would want to complete the correspondence they'd started that morning, picked up her shorthand book and pencil in readiness.

Leaning back in his chair, he flicked her a quick glance and began to dictate without preamble, but this time Cassie had no difficulty in keeping apace with him, her pencil skimming rapidly across the pages. It was certainly no great hardship listening to the deep-timbred, well modulated voice, she mused, recalling the monotonous tones of some of her past employers. In fact, she admitted grudgingly, she had a feeling that Adam Merrick could make the telephone directory sound fascinating if he so chose.

Uncharacteristically, he suddenly broke off in midsentence. Pencil poised, Cassie waited expectantly for him to continue, wondering vaguely what had broken his train of thought so abruptly.

'Have we ever met before?'

Startled, she jerked her head up, and was further disconcerted to discover the blue eyes resting intently on her face. What was this? she wondered, instantly suspicious. The prelude to another wind-up? Of course they'd never met before.

She gave a careless shrug. 'No. At least not that I can recall,' she murmured glibly, refusing to pamper to his over-inflated male ego by being more positive. It was galling enough to have to admit to herself that if she had ever encountered this man before, however briefly, it would have been printed indelibly in her subconscious forever. 'But then I have the most appalling memory for names and faces,' she added for good measure, and wondered if she'd slightly overdone it. Not that it mattered, she thought drily, as he didn't appear to have heard a word she'd said anyway.

Her hackles began to rise as he continued to survey her with cool, clinical detachment. There wasn't the slightest flicker of warmth in his eyes, no acknowledgment that she was even human let alone a woman, she thought with searing resentment. It was as if she were some sort of mathematical puzzle that needed solving.

'You remind me of someone,' he drawled finally, eyebrows knitting in a pensive dark line across his forehead.

Cassie stiffened, her fingers tightening unconsciously around her pencil. It wasn't possible... Could he really have noticed a resemblance? She tensed, shaken and dismayed by the intensity of the hope that engulfed her. Was that recognition she'd once craved more than anything in the world still so important to her? Schooling her features into an impassive mask, she flicked an upward glance. 'Well, they say that everyone has a double,' she said shortly.

'It's not an obvious likeness. Something far more elusive.' Thoughtfully he rubbed a lean hand across his square chin. 'When you were laughing earlier on...' He shook his head as if trying to dislodge a dormant memory, and then his eyes darkened dismissively, rejecting her as if she were some inanimate object in an auction which, on closer scrutiny, he was no longer interested in purchasing.

'Read that last sentence back to me, please.'

Cassie bent over her notebook. Not an obvious likeness... It was ridiculous to feel so deflated, she told herself roughly, absurd to feel so cheated and disappointed. It wasn't as if it mattered any more... Concentrate, she ordered herself firmly and, focusing her eyes on her shorthand, began to read out loud.

Aware of the growing gloom outside, Cassie stretched out an arm and switched on the light switch behind her desk. Adam Merrick might possess eyes like a cat, but she didn't. Her gaze rested briefly on the bowed dark head. Didn't the click of the typewriter distract him from reading that large pile of papers in front of him? Or did he simply block it out as effectively as he seemed to have blocked out her own presence in the room? Since completing his dictation he hadn't addressed one word to her, hadn't to her knowledge even glanced at her.

She shook herself mentally, irritated and slightly perturbed by her illogical chagrin. Mechanically she inserted a fresh sheet of paper into the typewriter and frowned. Was that clock on the wall right?

'Professor Merrick?'

'Hmm?'

Cassie's lips compressed together. It would be nice to address a face instead of a head. 'It's nearly four o'clock.'

He raised his eyes from the table and surveyed her speculatively. 'Thank you for sharing that with me, Cassandra.'

Very funny. 'William,' she said brusquely, and felt a rush of exasperation as he continued to regard her with mild curiosity.

'Your nephew? Remember?' How could he have forgotten all about the small boy? 'Wouldn't he be waiting to be picked up from school?' she demanded icily. As she saw the shutters slam down over the blue eyes, she instinctively braced herself for a rebuff and was nonplussed when he merely shrugged his broad shoulders.

'I've already arranged for him to be collected. In fact he should be delivered any minute now.' He bowed his head back over his desk.

Delivered? Cassie recoiled from the complete and utter indifference both in his voice and attitude. He was talking about a child, for heaven's sake, not a parcel. What a life for William, she thought with heated compassion, stuck day after day with this cold-blooded excuse for a human being.

She heard the slamming of a door and then the sound of small running footsteps. My God, he hadn't even glanced up, Cassie thought in disbelief, scowling ferociously at the bowed head. The next minute the study door burst open and William tore into the room like a miniature whirlwind, his small face aglow with excitement and pride.

'I'm going to be a shepherd instead of a donkey.' He beamed at his uncle and then smiled shyly at Cassie, who grinned back warmly. School Christmas play? Her eyes flew to Adam Merrick. If he squashed the boy, laughed . . .

'That's wonderful, William.'

Incredulously, Cassie registered the genuine enthusiasm in the deep voice, saw the pleasure on the small boy's face as he basked in his uncle's approval.

'Are Tommy and Peter still shepherds?'

Her incredulity intensifying, Cassie listened as Adam Merrick began to discuss the play with as much seriousness as if it were a new West End production. He was obviously familiar with every child in William's class, knew exactly which part each was to take in the forthcoming nativity play.

'Was wondering 'bout Lisa,' William murmured thoughtfully. 'Shepherds always have dogs, don't they? I could ask Mrs Anderson if it was all right to bring her.'

'Mmm.' Adam Merrick nodded with equal thoughtfulness. 'Do you think it would be very fair on Lisa? She might get very frightened,' he said gently.

'S'pose so,' William agreed and swung around to face Cassie. 'It came out,' he announced with careless pride and, digging deep into his pocket, retrieved a small white milk tooth carefully encased in a piece of tissue paper.

Cassie's mouth curved into a wide warm smile. 'You'll have to put it under your pillow tonight for the tooth fairy,' she murmured, and instantly recognised her *faux pas* as an expression of disgust crossed his face.

'The tooth fairy,' he scoffed. 'I'm nearly six!' he informed her severely. Then, relenting, he bestowed a forgiving smile upon her and moved across to his uncle.

Solemnly, Adam Merrick picked up the tooth from his nephew's outstretched palm, and placed a silver coin in its place. 'We've cut out the middle man,' he murmured drily over the top of the small head to Cassie. Dark blue eyes sought hers, inviting her to share his own suppressed amusement.

Cassie's lips curved into a stiff, unnatural smile, an illogical feeling of panic tingling down her spine as she

met his fleeting, conspiratorial glance. She didn't want
to start liking this man, didn't want to start believing
that he had any redeeming qualities at all.

He rose to his feet in a swift, fluid movement. 'Come
on, Will.' He rumpled the dark head. 'Go and change
out of your school clothes and we'll take Lisa for her
walk.' He herded his charge across the room. 'Oh, by
the way, Mrs Evans isn't very well so Cassandra is going
to look after you tonight.'

'Are you really?' the small boy demanded with
flattering enthusiasm, beaming at Cassie.

'Y-yes,' she agreed weakly, and smiled back at him,
refusing even to glance up at the towering figure behind
him. Game, set and match, Professor Merrick, although
your idea of fair play stinks!

'What shall we do now?' William gazed confidently at
Cassie across the kitchen table. The jigsaw that had occupied it hitherto had been completed and put away. 'I
usually play football with Uncle Adam before I go to
bed.'

'Football?' Cassie said dubiously, looking down into
the guileless blue eyes. The physical resemblance between uncle and nephew was very pronounced, almost
uncanny. 'Outside?' It was pitch-black...

'In the hall.' He suddenly looked guilty. 'That's how
he hurt his wrist. Diving to save one of my goals.'

Cassie turned round to hide her wide grin of amused
delight as a vision of Adam Merrick throwing himself
to the ground in his goalkeeper routine sprang vividly
into her head. Automatically she glanced upwards as she
heard the sound of firm footsteps in the overhead
bathroom. No wonder he'd never actually mentioned
how he'd injured his wrist! No wonder, too, that the hall
was bare of pictures and ornaments if it was habitually
used as a soccer pitch—doubtlessly after the housekeeper had left for the day!

'I'll go and set up the goalposts and fetch the ball,' William informed her, evidently taking her silence for assent, and darted out of the kitchen. 'Come along,' he piped impatiently from the hall.

Cassie raised an eyebrow and rose to her feet. Apparently Merrick minor didn't just resemble his uncle physically.

'You can have first shot at goal,' William informed her graciously as she joined him in the hall. 'I'll move the goalposts too, make it a bit wider,' he added kindly.

'Thank you,' Cassie said gratefully. Strange how much those goalposts resembled wellington boots. She was beginning to feel haunted by them, would probably dream about them.

'We'll use the match ball today,' William announced, and with great reverence placed it in front of her. If she hadn't known otherwise, Cassie mused, she might have supposed it was a round sphere of rags tied up with string... Seeing that the goalkeeper had adopted an authoritative stance between the goalposts, she stepped back, was about to give the ball a hefty swipe with her foot, and faltered as she heard the explosive grunt of irritation.

She glanced up, her throat suddenly constricting as she saw Adam Merrick coming down the stairs towards her in full evening dress, dark eyebrows knitted together across his forehead.

'Can't tie this wretched thing!'

Cassie swallowed, his implication clear. Even if she had a clue how to tie a bowtie, she simply couldn't... He was looming over her, waiting expectantly.

'Um—I don't know how...' she muttered unsteadily, her sense of smell dominated by the scent of clean, soapy, male skin.

'Stand on the bottom stair,' he ordered. 'You'll be able to reach more easily from there.'

Steeling herself, she did as he asked and flinched inwardly. This was worse, her eyes were now in direct line with his. His pupils were dark, dilated... Her gaze dropped to the strand of silk draped around his collar.

'Right, pick up both ends and...'

She tried to concentrate on his instructions, tried to ignore his proximity, but every time her hand inadvertently brushed against his throat or the hard wall of his chest, her heart skipped a beat, her breathing growing more and more erratic. She forgot William, was oblivious to her surroundings, all her senses overpowered by the formidable masculine presence standing barely inches away from her. His maleness was like a concrete, tangible force, invading every pore in her body. And she hated it. Hated the feeling of being dominated against her will. Hated the feeling that she was no longer in complete control of herself. And most of all she hated the knowledge that this man could without a word, a glance or touch reduce her to this fumbling bundle of nerves.

'There you are, you shall go to the ball after all, Professor,' she murmured facetiously, her voice several octaves higher than usual as she finally completed her task. She flicked a glance upwards and her throat went dry. The blue eyes, darkened to navy beneath the sweep of jet black lashes, were fixed intently on the curve of her mouth. A pulse began to race at the base of her neck, the blood pounding in her head. He wouldn't dare. Especially not with William present. She took a step backwards and, forgetting she was perched on the lower stair, lost her balance and slid elegantly on to her bottom.

There was a chortle of laughter from William.

'Are you all right?' his uncle drawled smoothly.

'Perfectly,' she snapped, her voice unsteady. Ignoring the lean outstretched hand, she scrambled to her feet, overwhelmingly relieved when the chime of the doorbell diverted her unwanted audience's attention away from herself.

Hand on the banister, she watched Adam Merrick stride across to the door. He'd been playing another of

his power games, she thought savagely. Instead of over-
reacting like a terrified rabbit, she should have stood her
ground, called his bluff. And if he had carried out his
wordless threat... Tiny goosebumps prickled down her
spine.

'Taxi to Tanworth Hall, sir,' she heard the figure in
the porch murmur.

'Thank you.' Adam Merrick glanced back over his
shoulder. 'Be good, Will.' There was an almost imperceptible pause. 'Goodnight, Cassandra.' The door
slammed firmly behind him.

Taking a deep, controlling breath, Cassie descended
the one stair to the hall, her pulse-rate slowly returning
to normal. So Adam Merrick was attending the same
charity function tonight as Kate and Richard and, presumably, was collecting his dinner companion *en route*.
Unbidden the image of Adam Merrick, smiling deep into
the eyes of a shadowy, beautiful woman, her arm linked
possessively through his, crept insidiously into her head.
Unconsciously her forehead furrowed into a scowl. The
faceless, nameless woman was welcome to him!

'Are you OK? I mean you're not still cross because I
laughed at you? I didn't really mean to. But you just
looked so funny.'

The treble voice broke through her reverie, snapped
her with a guilty start back to the present.

'Of course I'm not cross.' She smiled down into the
small, worried face.

'Want to go on playing football, then?' William enquired hopefully.

Unable to resist the plea in the blue eyes, Cassie
nodded.

After suffering crashing defeats at both football and
Snap, she ran William's bath and prepared him for bed.
Clad in blue and white pyjamas, he snuggled down into
his sheets and looked up at her. 'Will you read me a
story? About Pooh Bear?'

Smiling her assent, Cassie moved across to the bookcase and extracted the well-worn edition of the children's classic. Carrying it back across the room, she sat down on the edge of the bed, gave a cursory glance at the framed photograph on William's bedside table and jolted. A younger, less severe Adam Merrick was looking down with possessive pride at the slim dark-haired girl by his side. It was as if her earlier imagining had somehow conjured up a reality.

'That's my Mummy and Daddy.' William's calm, matter-of-fact voice penetrated her confused thoughts.

'But?' Cassie muttered in complete bewilderment.

'Uncle Adam and my Daddy were twins.' Wriggling up in his bed, William reached out for the photograph and handed it to her for closer inspection.

Heart constricting with pity, Cassie's eyes moved slowly over the young woman to the man by her side. The superficial likeness between the twin brothers was very pronounced—she could see how easily she had jumped to the wrong conclusion—but there was a hint of weakness in the dark face looking up at her that was markedly absent in Adam Merrick's.

'Your Mummy was very lovely,' she said softly as she placed the photograph back on the table.

William smiled and drew his knees up to his chest. 'Rowena,' he murmured, drawing the word out with great deliberation almost as if he were committing it to memory. 'She had a pretty name, too, didn't she?' His fingers began to pick the corner of his sheet. 'I like talking about Mummy and Daddy.'

Cassie nodded slowly. She'd had the same need to talk about her parents as a child. A need that Kate, unlike every other adult, who had shied away from the subject, had seemed intuitively to understand.

'Uncle Adam tells me stories about Daddy sometimes...' William stopped, looked at Cassie uncertainly and then, seemingly reassured by something in her eyes, continued, 'But when I talk about Mummy he gets...not cross 'xactly...' He paused, forehead creasing, as if trying to conjure up a word from his limited five-year-old's vocabulary. 'Just sort of funny,' he finished lamely and then, his face clearing, he smiled. 'Will you read about Pooh Bear now?'

Beginning to feel slightly out of her depth, Cassie felt a wave of shamed relief as William wriggled back down to his bed and looked up at her expectantly. She picked up the book lying on her lap, and began to read the familiar words out loud. It was odd that Adam Merrick evidently found it easier, less painful, to talk about his twin brother than his sister-in-law, she mused absently. As William's eyelids began to grow heavy, flicker downwards, she quietly closed the book.

'I like you. You smell nice,' he murmured sleepily as she tucked in the bedclothes.

'I like you too, William,' Cassie said softly, aching to pick him up in her arms and hug him. He was so small, so vulnerable. 'Goodnight.'

'Night.' He suddenly swept back the bedclothes and launched himself into her arms, making her instantly regret her reticence. He was only five years old, little more than a baby despite all his self-composure. Of course he needed a bedtime cuddle.

Settling him back down into bed, she kissed his soft cheek and moved across the carpet to the door. 'See you in the morning. Sleep well.' She'd only known the small boy a few hours and yet she was already becoming dangerously attached to him, she realised with an uneasy jolt. Flicking off the light, she made her way back downstairs.

She made a cup of coffee, carried it through into the sitting-room and set it down on a small polished wooden table. Then, kicking off her shoes, she padded across the thick, russet carpet, drawn to the display of photographs arrayed on the windowsill in the far corner of the room. Several school snaps of a self-conscious, grinning William. One of his paternal grandparents—

the family likeness between the tall, lean, distinguished grey-haired man, a serene smiling woman by his side, and his progeny was all too apparent. Two photographs of William's father. On his own... Cassie's eyes darkened, puzzled by the obvious omission. The absence of Rowena Merrick's presence in the small family gallery was very marked, seemed almost pointed, and one that William surely could not have failed to notice.

Thoughtfully Cassie picked up her coffee and settled down on the chintz-covered sofa, tucking her slim legs up beside her. Whatever her reservations about Adam Merrick, she was forced to admit that his relationship with his nephew appeared to be an excellent one. That his small charge seemed to be so happy and well-adjusted had to be attributable to him. Which made it even more baffling that he should apparently be so insensitive about such an important issue as William's mother.

A huge yawn engulfed her. She still hadn't brought in her overnight bag from the car, she reminded herself. Would do that in a minute. She yawned again. Then have a long, hot soak in the bath...

Cassie's eyelashes flickered upwards and she frowned. She could hear footsteps in the hall—voices... Her eyes flew to her wristwatch. It was only half-past ten. What was he doing home this early? She jerked herself upright and ran a hand through her tumbled red curls. There had been two voices, one male and one quite definitely female... Great, she mused sourly. Never at her best in the morning, the last thing she wanted tomorrow was to have to make polite conversation to some unknown woman over the breakfast table.

She thrust her feet into her shoes. Although, come to think of it, now Adam Merrick was back so early it seemed fatuous her staying the night anyway. She might just as well go home to Mead Cottage right now. Doubtless under the circumstances he would be as relieved by her departure as she would be herself.

Crossing the carpet, she entered the hall. Judging from the light issuing from the open doorway, they were in the kitchen. She began to walk briskly towards it and then stopped dead, her mind whirling with shocked disbelief. Adam Merrick was leaning back against the sink unit, his arms folded tightly around the slim woman resting her dark head against his shoulder. Impossible. It couldn't be . . . Kate!

CHAPTER FIVE

'I'M all right now. Thanks, Adam.'

Transfixed, Cassie watched Kate raise her head from the broad shoulder, her shock changing to concerned bewilderment as she saw the tearstains on her aunt's cheek. Kate never cried... There must be something dreadfully wrong for her to look so distressed.

Instinctively Cassie started to take a step forward and then halted. If Kate had wanted to talk to her, she would have come and found her. Had her aunt had some terrible argument with Richard... and sought solace in the arms of a virtual stranger, a man she'd only met a few hours ago? It simply didn't make sense. She shouldn't be standing here like a voyeur. Any minute now Adam Merrick might glance up and see her. She ought to say something, make her presence felt... Swiftly Cassie turned away, crept silently back along the hall, tiptoed up the stairs and bolted into the spare bedroom at the far end of the landing.

Switching on the bedroom lamp, she walked over to the sash window, gazed out into the darkness for a moment and then drew the soft peach curtains together. She'd wanted Kate to find another man, she thought with mounting hysteria. But Kate and Adam Merrick...

She threw herself down in the wicker chair and kicked off her shoes, making tiny circles in the deep-pile cream carpet with her toes. It simply wasn't in Kate's nature to walk out on one man and go careering off with another. Maybe that was a bit over-dramatic. But of all the men in the world, to pick on Adam Merrick...

Jumping to her feet, she tugged off her sweatshirt and sighed. Her overnight bag was still in the car, the keys of which were on a hook in the kitchen. Why was she

77

acting so unnaturally? Why hadn't she simply gone into the kitchen and greeted her aunt the moment she'd seen her? Because she'd been flustered, thrown off balance. Seeing her aunt wrapped around her employer wasn't quite what she'd expected! It was incomprehensible. It simply was not Kate!

She stripped off the rest of her clothes, grateful now that she'd made up the bed earlier with clean linen and placed towels in the small but well-appointed en-suite bathroom.

Padding into the bathroom, she opened the wall cabinet without much hope and was pleasantly surprised to discover a new bar of soap and a tube of toothpaste. Probably had Adam Merrick's housekeeper to thank for that. Showering quickly, a long leisurely bath no longer appealing, she brushed her teeth and, wrapped in a soft, white bath-towel returned to the bedroom. Picking up her jeans from the floor where she'd tossed them, remembering with a wry smile how she'd gently admonished William earlier for doing the exact same thing, she laid them neatly over the back of the wicker chair and then, discarding her towel, scrambled into bed. She switched off the bedside lamp and, arms folded behind her head, stared up into the darkness. She'd made a mistake. It simply could not have been Kate locked in Adam Merrick's arms...

Despite her conviction to the contrary she fell into a deep, dreamless sleep and woke to find sunlight filtering into the room beneath the curtains. Momentarily disorientated, recollection returned swiftly and she scrambled out of bed.

She blinked at her wristwatch, cursed as she realised she'd forgotten to wind it up last night and padded into the bathroom, cursing again as she stubbed her bare toe on the corner of the bath. Showering swiftly, she scowled at her worn underclothes and, ignoring them, pulled on her sweatshirt and jeans. Priority number one was to collect her overnight case. Raking a hand through her tumbled red-gold curls, she caught sight of her glowering face in the mirror and stuck out a childish tongue. Hell. Anyone would feel a bit disgruntled at the thought of starting the day without clean underwear and a comb. Slamming the door behind her, she walked swiftly along the length of the landing and down the stairs.

Making her way along the hall, she pushed open the kitchen door and faltered. Adam Merrick, clad in a white towelling robe, was sitting at the table, whistling under his breath, a newspaper propped up in front of him.

Cassie gave his bowed head a baleful glare. Did he have to be so impossibly cheerful first thing in the morning? And for Pete's sake, would it have killed the dratted man to have dressed before coming down to breakfast?

'Good morning,' he greeted her easily, glancing up. 'Tea in the pot,' he added laconically.

'Thanks,' she grunted, trying to ignore the expanse of tanned chest, liberally covered with fine dark hairs, revealed at the V of the robe, the tang of recently soaped male skin mixed with the subtle fragrance of expensive aftershave. He'd evidently managed to wield the razor himself this morning, she registered subconsciously. His hair, still damp from the shower, sprang in unruly dark waves over his head and she was appalled by her desire to curl her fingers through the rich thickness. In the same instant she was suddenly conscious of his own blatant masculine appraisal, knew without a doubt from the unashamedly appreciative glint in his eyes that he was fully conversant with the fact that she wasn't wearing a bra.

To her shamed, helpless horror she felt her nipples tauten, a burning, teasing warmth taunting the very core of her being. The whole of her ungovernable body was responding with humiliating, wilful abandonment to the flagrant male gaze.

'Have you seen my car keys?' It took every ounce of self-control to keep her voice steady, to meet the fully-aware, dark blue eyes without flinching. 'I left them on the hook.'

'Katherine took the car home this morning,' he drawled.

'Kate's been here...' she began, feigning surprise, and snapped her mouth closed as he raised a sceptical dark eyebrow. He'd seen her last night standing outside the kitchen door. She must have looked so absurd creeping furtively away...

'She came up to see you before she left but you were still fast asleep.' Muffling a yawn, he stretched his arms up indolently above his head, hard muscle straining the shoulders of the robe, causing it to gape over the deep, powerful chest.

Damn exhibitionist, Cassie thought savagely, her stomach knotting. She forced her legs to move to a chair and sank into it.

He smiled at her blandly across the table. 'Would you like the heating turned up?' he enquired solicitously.

Cassie smiled back. Bastard. 'Thank you,' she returned sweetly, eyelashes shielding her gaze as she watched him move with fluid, feral grace across to the thermostat on the wall. His calves were well-muscled, matted with silky dark hairs. Swiftly averting her gaze as he turned round, Cassie picked up the teapot with an unsteady hand and filled her mug. Gratefully she took a long sip and froze. *Kate had driven home this morning.* Adam's words simply hadn't registered until now. Or had she simply blocked her mind to them, heard what she'd chosen to hear rather than what he'd actually said? She stared down into her tea. OK, so Kate had spent the night here. So what? It didn't automatically mean... No point in rushing to rash conclusions... She simply couldn't believe that Kate and a total stranger...

'Help yourself to toast. Cereal. Eggs,' Adam Merrick murmured as he rejoined her at the table.

'Thank you,' she said automatically, the thought of food making her stomach churn even more. 'Um—where's William?' she asked stiffly.

'Kate dropped him off at school on her way.' He replenished his own mug of tea from the pot and then smiled. 'It was a hell of a surprise seeing her again last night.'

Cassie's eyes jerked to his face. 'You know her... I mean you've met before?'

'Kate was at university with Andrew. My brother. They were very close for a while.'

'Kate and your brother?' Cassie echoed in disbelief, her eyes widening.

'Mmm. In fact——' he paused, a muscle flickering along the length of his jaw '—they even talked about getting married.'

Cassie surveyed him warily from under her eyelashes, confused by the inexplicable note of bitterness in his voice, the expression in the dark blue shadowy depths of his eyes. Not the understandable pain that talking about his twin might induce, but something else. But the expression was too fleeting, frustratingly impossible to analyse.

'So what happened?' she prompted quietly. She was doubtless being inordinately insensitive, would be wiser to let the matter drop, but she needed badly to know the answer to why Kate's romance had come to an end. If the reason was as she suspected, Kate wouldn't tell her the truth. And besides, she assuaged her twinge of guilt, it was Adam, after all, who had instigated the conversation about Kate and Andrew... She frowned. When had she suddenly started thinking of him as Adam...?

For a moment she thought he wasn't going to reply, hadn't even heard, and then he shrugged, his dark face now completely bland.

'They were both very young. People change,' he murmured. 'I suppose they just started to drift apart.'

When Kate moved away from London and down to Mead Cottage with me, Cassie finished silently. The single, unattached Kate Richardson must have been a very different proposition from the one encumbered with an nine-year-old dependent. Although she would hardly expect Adam to admit that was why his brother had ditched Kate.

He smiled. 'I've actually spoken to Kate on the phone but it still didn't occur to me to make the connection. I suppose——'

'The last thing you ever expected was to find her running a secretarial agency in a small country town,' Cassie finished for him shortly. She knew that Kate's chief motive in buying Mead Cottage and starting her own business was that she could work from home, thus eliminating the need for child-minders for her young niece. Cassie's eyes darkened. Whenever she had come home from school, whenever she'd been ill, during the holidays, Kate had always been there...

'She must have only been about twenty-two when...' mused the deep voice thoughtfully.

'Yes,' Cassie agreed gruffly. At twenty-two Kate had sacrificed her career and possibly marriage to take care of her small niece. Whereas at exactly the same age, she was floating aimlessly from job to job, place to place... She could feel the blue eyes resting on her face and knew that he too must be making the comparison in his mind.

'She's a very special lady,' he murmured quietly. He was silent for a second, his expression unreadable, and then, draining his mug, he rose briskly to his feet. 'I'm going up to London this morning. You'll find plenty of work in the study. I've left instructions on the dicta-phone.' He flicked a glance at his watch. 'I'd like to catch the five past ten.'

Presumably that was an indirect order to his chauffeur, Cassie thought acidly, watching him move across the kitchen. And presumably she was in his employ for another day. She frowned. If Kate had the car...

'We'll use mine,' he drawled over his shoulder before disappearing into the hall.

What was he? Cassie pulled a face at the closed door. A flipping thought reader? A twinge of unease tingled through her. It wasn't the first time she'd had the uncanny sensation that he was reading her thoughts. It was something she would have to watch.

Cassie's eyes slid to her passenger as she guided the powerful red estate car along the road. Was he going to keep up that incessant soft whistling for the whole journey? It was beginning to get on her nerves. He looked so damn cheerful, sitting there with that smug, Cheshire Cat expression on his face. As if he were recalling some exceedingly delightful memory. Her stomach muscles clenched.

As soon as she dropped Adam off at the station she would race back to Mead Cottage and change into some fresh clothes. Probably stop and have a quick coffee with Kate. The knot in her stomach tightened. It was absurd to feel so apprehensive, almost awkward, about seeing the person with whom she normally felt most comfortable in all the world.

Turning left, she drew into the station yard and came to a halt, eyes focused directly ahead as she waited for Adam to get out. As he made no move to do so, she flicked him a sideways glance and found his eyes resting speculatively on her face.

'Why didn't you tell me yesterday that Liselle Maurice was your mother?'

Caught completely off guard by the abrupt question, Cassie tensed, eyelashes dropping instinctively over her eyes. Liselle Maurice. The beautiful, talented actress whose tragic death had exalted her to almost legendary status. Lisa Richardson. Her mother. One and the same person and yet in her mind they had always had two separate identities. 'Kate?' she muttered stiffly and, as he gave an affirmative nod, felt a sweep of curious re-

sentiment that Adam and Kate had discussed her without
her knowledge.

'So?' he prompted quietly. 'Why didn't you tell me?'

Because I didn't want to see the disbelief on your face,
she thought. 'Was there any reason why I should have?'
she enquired frigidly.

'I actually met her a couple of times. Through Kate,'
he said softly, almost as if she hadn't spoken. 'She was
exquisite.'

Cassie swallowed, her eyes focused unseeingly ahead
as she heard the undisguised admiration and respect in
his voice. How Liselle Maurice could have produced such
a plain, unprepossessing child... Clenching her jaw,
Cassie pushed the remembered words roughly back into
her subconscious. For heaven's sake, why was she being
so inordinately sensitive today? OK, maybe the ugly
duckling hadn't exactly turned into the proverbial swan,
but she'd turned into a pretty presentable duck! She
flicked Adam a quick sideways glance from under her
long lashes. And he had noticed some resemblance,
however slight... 'You said yesterday,' she said with
feigned casualness before she could stop herself, 'that I
reminded you...'

She could have bitten off her tongue as she saw the
immediate gleam in his eyes, cursed herself inwardly for
her stupidity, wondering what on earth had possessed
her to make herself such an easy prey.

'Fishing, Miss Richardson?' he drawled.

'Not my hobby,' she snapped back, forcing herself to
meet the taunting blue eyes without flinching. 'I'm anti
all blood sports.'

With a low mocking laugh, he reached for the door-
handle and swung himself out. With narrowed eyes,
Cassie watched him lope with long, fluid strides towards
the station entrance. Clad in dark, expertly tailored
trousers and a black cashmere sweater, a leather jacket
slung casually over his shoulder, he looked tough and
uncompromisingly male, a man equipped to deal with

every physical as well as mental challenge that came his way.

Without warning, Cassie's stomach gave a sickening lurch as she faced the unpalatable truth. She'd wanted Adam to see more than a superficial fleeting likeness between herself and Liselle Maurice, not because of some long-dormant childhood hang-up, but because she'd wanted his tacit admission that she was an equally attractive, desirable woman. She wanted just for one second to see the undisguised male admiration in his eyes that she'd witnessed when he spoke of both Kate and her mother. Cringing inwardly, warmth seeping through her body, firing her cheeks with colour, she recalled the mockery in the taunting blue eyes. How could she have been so obvious... ? The warmth ebbed from her body, an icy cold finger trickling down her spine. From the first moment she'd laid eyes on Adam Merrick, she'd been reacting to him, not as an employee to an employer, but first and foremost as a woman to a man, some hitherto dormant feminine core deep within her recognising and responding with primeval instinct to his latent virility.

Ignoring the tightness in her chest, Cassie took a deep breath, refusing to submit to the panic that threatened to engulf her completely. After today, there was no reason at all why she should ever encounter Adam Merrick again. Unless, of course, he and Kate... With a sudden unladylike epithet, she slammed her palms down on the steering-wheel, saw the startled expression on the face of an elderly passer-by and grinned self-consciously back.

Switching on the ignition she swung the car round, forcing herself to concentrate on her driving as she merged with the busy main road. She joined the dual carriageway and then impulsively turned off on to a slip road, deciding to follow the more scenic route through the outskirts of the New Forest back to Mead Cottage.

As she crossed a cattle grid in the road she reduced her speed, keeping a vigilant watch out for the free-roaming ponies, donkeys and cattle that might without warning step out in front of the car. Unable to resist, she drew on to the verge for a few moments and watched a pig snuffling beneath a massive oak tree, optimistically rooting in the frosty ground for any remaining acorns. Winding down the window, Cassie inhaled the cold, crisp, pine-scented air, stretched her arms above her head and gazed up at the azure sky as she let the tension ease from her body. Perhaps she'd persuade Kate to come for a long hike on Sunday, maybe stop off and have lunch in a country pub—unless of course Kate had made other plans for Sunday.

Eyebrows knitted together, Cassie closed the window, turned on the heater full blast and moved off, arriving back at Mead Cottage some ten minutes later.

'Hello, Mary. Feeling better?' she greeted the receptionist as she pushed open the agency door.

'Much, thanks. And how are you? You must tell me all about Australia—some other time,' she added wryly as the telephone began to ring. 'Kate's free at the moment...' she mouthed.

Cassie nodded and walked across the carpet towards the inner office. She paused, staring at the closed door, chewing her bottom lip. Then taking a deep breath she entered the office, discovering her aunt in the tiny kitchenette, pouring boiling water into a mug.

'Morning, Cass.' Kate smiled over her shoulder. 'Coffee?'

'Thanks.' Cassie grinned. 'I left something in your car...just popped back to fetch it.' Her grin broadened. 'Isn't it a heavenly day? Much too good to be indoors...' She stopped, aware of how unnatural she sounded, aware too of Kate's thoughtful gaze resting on her over-animated face.

'I was going to phone you later.' Kate handed her a mug and then moved over to her desk and sat down.

'Two more of my regular staff have gone down with flu today, so I was wondering how you felt about carrying on at Adam's for the time being.'

Her heart plummeting, Cassie sank into the chair beside the desk, her hands tightening round her mug. 'Fine,' she said casually, long thick lashes shielding her apprehensive eyes. The last thing in the world she wanted was to go on working for Adam Merrick. She could feel that illogical surge of panic rising up in her again and fought it back down. But how could she refuse to help Kate out when the agency's resources were obviously stretched to the full at the moment? Her reluctance was completely irrational anyway, she told herself ferociously. OK, so she wasn't as completely immune to Adam Merrick as she would have wished, but it was nothing she couldn't handle. It wasn't as if he presented any emotional threat! Besides, she would have had to start looking for temporary employment soon anyway, so surely working for Adam Merrick was as good a stopgap as any? She looked up at Kate. 'Did you have a good time last night?' she asked abruptly.

'Mmm. I did.' Kate took a sip of coffee and then put her mug down. 'Oh, Cass, it was such a shock seeing Adam again after all these years. For a moment I thought it was Andrew...' Her voice trailed off.

Cassie's constraint evaporated. This was Kate, the person she loved most in the world, to whom she could talk about anything. 'Adam told me about you and Andrew.' She paused. 'Did you love him very much?' she asked gently.

'I suppose I must have thought so once,' Kate murmured slowly, her eyes pensive. 'But looking back I'm not so sure. We disagreed about a lot of things.' She shook her head. 'It was such a long time ago now.' She paused for a moment, her voice not quite steady as she continued. 'I couldn't believe it when Adam told me about the accident.' She lapsed into a long silence and then smiled up at Cassie. 'It was good to see Adam again, though. In many ways I used to get on much better with him than Andrew. Although they were so physically alike, their characters were very different.'

'Perhaps you became involved with the wrong brother,' Cassie said lightly. 'More coffee?' Abruptly she reached across the table to take Kate's mug and accidentally knocked it flying. It landed unharmed on the floor. 'Sorry,' Cassie murmured, stooping down to retrieve it. She rose to her feet and moved across to the kitchenette and, swilling both mugs, switched the kettle back on. A new thought suddenly stuck her. 'Didn't Richard mind you leaving with Adam?' she asked curiously over her shoulder. She'd forgotten all about Richard until now. Perhaps she'd been wrong about him after all . . . perhaps Kate did genuinely regard him as no more than a friend. Which meant that she was completely uninvolved emotionally.

'I didn't exactly leave with Adam,' Kate said drily, swivelling round in her chair. 'Richard wanted to leave early as he wasn't feeling well, probably coming down with this flu bug, and offered Adam a lift home. I think Adam was quite glad to leave by then.' She grinned. 'Apparently he's number one eligible bachelor in the area. He was hunted down last night by virtually every matron there with a daughter of marriageable age. Real Jane Austen stuff. And most of them were wearing that wish-I-were-twenty-years-younger expression on their faces.'

'He probably lapped it up,' Cassie muttered sourly, and saw Kate raise an eyebrow.

'Anyway, Richard dropped me off at Adam's so I could collect my car. Adam had already suggested that you use his for the time being.' Kate stretched her arms above her head and yawned. 'Adam's sofa is quite definitely not the most comfortable place to spend the night.' She grimaced, pressing a hand to the small of her back. 'Still it serves me right for falling asleep, I suppose.'

Studying her aunt surreptitiously under her lashes, Cassie carried the mugs back to the desk. She wished she were more of an expert on body language. Kate sounded so casual, so unconcerned... 'What I don't understand is why you and Adam didn't make the connection before now.' She wrinkled her nose thoughtfully. 'I suppose Richardson is a fairly common name but Merrick is more unusual. Didn't it make you even wonder?'

'Cass, the last time I saw Adam was at his engagement party, heaven knows how long ago now. I hadn't thought of him or Andrew for years. When a Professor Merrick phoned up the agency, no, it simply didn't occur to me that it could possibly be the boy I'd known so long ago. After all, the odds against it must be pretty high.'

'S'pose.' Cassie drained her mug, not wholly convinced that Kate was telling the entire truth. She couldn't quite believe that the name Merrick hadn't triggered off some memory in Kate's head—but perhaps it had been one that she'd preferred to forget and had quite deliberately chosen not to make the connection. She stiffened as the full implication of Kate's words hit her.

'Adam's engagement party?' she said slowly. 'But I thought he was a bachelor... I mean I didn't know he'd been married...'

'He hasn't,' Kate said quietly. 'Rowena jilted him three weeks before the wedding.'

'Rowena! But...'

'Yes. She married Andrew a few months later.'

Cassie jolted with shock. 'Rowena was engaged to Adam... and married Andrew?' she said incredulously. A double betrayal. By the woman he had loved enough to commit himself to for life. And his own twin brother. And now some tragic, ironic quirk of fate had left him responsible for their son. From a long way away she heard the telephone ring.

'I've a client waiting in Reception,' Kate murmured resignedly as she replaced the receiver.

'Right,' Cassie mumbled, her expression distant. Rising to her feet she walked across to the connecting door that led up to the flat. 'See you later.'

She collected Kate's car keys from the hook in the hall and, leaving the flat by the back entrance, went to retrieve her overnight bag and carried it back to her bedroom.

Changing into a clean pair of jeans and sweatshirt, she sat down in front of the dressing-table, brushed her hair and as an afterthought applied her rarely used lipstick. Was Rowena the reason Adam had never married? His reluctance to talk about her to William seemed to indicate that, even after all these years, the wound still had not healed. Blotting her lips carefully, she gazed unseeingly at her reflection. Had Adam attended his wedding? Endured seeing Andrew and Rowena together at every family gathering over the years...? She tried to ignore the compassion swelling up inside her, didn't want to feel anything, not even sympathy, for Adam Merrick.

Slipping her shoes on, she gave the room a quick cursory glance, and made her way back downstairs to the car park. Back to Welly Boot Cottage, she ordered herself briskly, swinging out into the road. Kate and Andrew...Adam and Rowena...Andrew and Rowena. Deliberately Cassie switched on the radio but the music failed to hold her concentration, refused to block out the jumble of names spinning around in her head like a merry-go-round. Perhaps she'd been right in her flippant remark that Kate had chosen the wrong brother, perhaps fate had now given both her and Adam a second chance. Ignoring the cramping sensation in the pit of her stomach, she drew up in front of the red-brick cottage.

It seemed impossible to believe that she'd only entered Adam Merrick's home for the first time barely twenty-four hours ago, she reflected as she pushed open the back door and walked in. Already it seemed completely familiar.

'Good girl, Lisa,' she murmured as the dog rose from its basket and inspected her carefully, feeling an illogical glow of warmth as it slowly wagged its tail.

Moving across the kitchen, she went into the hall. The sound of a hoover issued from the sitting-room. Emily, she thought wryly, correct in her assumption as the tiny woman popped her head around the door, nodded wordlessly and vanished back into the room.

Entering the study, Cassie settled down at her desk. Beside the dictaphone lay a large thick folder. She flicked it open and groaned inwardly as she quickly scanned the closely typed pages, noting the amendments in the margin. The learned tome, she mused gloomily. Sooner or later she'd known it was going to be inflicted upon her. Presumably Adam had made all the handwritten revisions to the manuscript before he'd sprained his wrist. Oh, well, she wasn't being paid to be entertained. Surely he wasn't expecting her to copy-type the whole sleep-inducing manuscript today?

Her eyes wandered around the room and she frowned. It was in exactly the same state of chaos as yesterday and yet it seemed different this morning. Lifeless. Sterile. Cold. Silent. Yet she could feel the heat emanating from the radiator behind her, hear the hum of the vacuum cleaner in the distance...

Picking up the earphones, she switched on the dictaphone, her gaze flicking automatically to the large oak desk as she heard the disembodied deep male voice in her ear. The clarity with which she could visualise its owner sitting behind the desk, long legs stretched out in front of him, hands folded with deceptive indolence behind his head, shook her profoundly.

He must have dealt with the morning's mail before she was up, she realised as he begun to dictate a letter. It sounded as if he had been invited to go on a lecture tour to Canada next summer.

Next summer... Her eyes darkened. Where would she be then? Rewinding the tape, she inserted some paper into the typewriter and concentrated on the familiar deep voice.

The correspondence complete, she removed the earphones and stretched her arms above her head, wiggling her fingers.

'Two-minute break,' she murmured, inclining her head towards the oak desk. 'Dock my pay if you like,' she added carelessly. Inserting a fresh sheet of paper into the typewriter, she set the margins and line spacing according to the very precise instructions on the tape and, opening the file by her side, set to work. Right. Chapter one...

Chapter fifteen. Cassie's eyes raced swiftly over the sheet in front of her, the typewriter inert by her side. She turned over the page impatiently. History had been her least favourite subject at school. If only she'd been given books like this to read, maybe she would have felt differently. Eighteenth-century England as seen through the eyes of two children from widely different social backgrounds came vividly to life before her. It was a fascinating, compelling insight into a period of history which, until now, she had thought of merely in terms of events and dates. If the author's intention had been to inspire the layman to research further into the period, he had succeeded. She was filled with a desire to rush out and read every book she could find about the eighteenth century, wanted to discover more about the architecture, the literature, the politics and most of all the day-to-day lives of the people of that era.

Frowning, she glanced up as she heard the sound of a car drawing up outside, and then blanched. He couldn't be home already! She flicked a quick glance at the clock, suddenly aware of the growing gloom in the room. It couldn't possibly be that late! She'd only intended reading a couple of pages. With increasing dismay she surveyed the small pile of newly typed sheets lying beside the much thicker folder. Professor Adam Merrick wasn't going to be over-impressed with her day's activity, she mused gloomily, looking back towards the taxi. She swallowed hard, disturbed by the way her heart somersaulted as the tall lean figure emerged from the black cab and strode up the path.

She heard the click of the front door, the sound of a joyous bark, and swiftly bent her head over the typewriter, fingers whizzing mechanically over the keyboard. She tensed as the study door opened, schooling her features into an impressive mask, and was shaken by the rush of pleasure that swept over her as she looked up into the dark, craggy face.

'How are you getting on?' he drawled, leaning against the door-jamb. 'Any problems?'

'Fine,' Cassie smiled blithely, wincing inwardly as she saw the perceptive blue gaze sweep over the revealing two piles of manuscript on her desk.

'Good.' He gave an approving smile which she instantly distrusted. 'I'm just going to change and then take Lisa for a quick walk before it gets dark. Fancy coming?'

For a moment Cassie was too startled by the casual invitation to answer. Had this sudden bonhomie something to do with the fact that he now knew her to be Kate's niece? Rapidly she gathered her wits. 'No, thanks. I'd prefer to get on,' she said stiffly, aware that it wasn't zealousness that had prompted her reply. Quite simply she didn't want to go for a casual afternoon stroll with this man, wanted their relationship to remain completely cool and impersonal, wanted to think of him simply as Professor Adam Merrick, her employer... No. She didn't want to think of him at all.

'Oh, come on, have a break. I'm sure you deserve one.' He smiled down at her. 'I expect you've been toiling over that hot typewriter all day.' Thoughtfully, he picked up the slim pile of papers that represented her day's work. 'Shouldn't think you even stopped for lunch, hmm?'

Sarcastic bastard. Berating herself soundly for being so easily duped yet again, Cassie raised her eyes challengingly to his face, prepared for battle. Blue eyes locked into grey for a brief second and then to her inexplicable disappointment, instead of launching into the expected caustic tirade, he gave a low mocking laugh and vanished into the hall.

'We aim to amuse,' Cassie muttered sourly, glaring at the closed door. Had he guessed just how she'd actually spent the greater part of her working day? If that were the case, then he had an extremely exalted view of his ability as a writer. She'd only been so enthusiastic about his book earlier because it hadn't been quite as tedious as she'd anticipated, that was all.

The sound of the doorbell cut across her reverie. She ignored it. The ringing became more insistent.

'Cassandra!' The deep bellow echoed down the hall.

Stretching her arms above her head, Cassie rose slowly to her feet, sauntered across the carpet and opened the door.

'You called?' she murmured sweetly.

'Answer that damn door!' growled a voice above her head.

Temper, temper, Professor. 'Yes, of course,' she answered with an obliging smile, and glanced upwards. The smile froze on her lips, her breath catching in her throat at the sight of the lean figure, apparently clad in nothing but a towel knotted around his hips, leaning over the landing banisters towards her. He must have decided to take a shower before changing. She swallowed convulsively as her eyes followed the line of fine dark hair that covered the deep chest, arrowed over the taut flat stomach and disappeared beneath the towel.

Swiftly she averted her gaze and, spinning round, marched to the front door, welcoming the sudden rush of cold air against her heated face as she flung it open.

She frowned. There was something familiar about the bespectacled girl standing there—of course, the student in the pub.

'Hello.' Cassie smiled encouragingly as the other girl surveyed her in total silence.

'Who are you?' she finally demanded bluntly, obviously having failed to recognise Cassie from the previous day.

'Ad...' Cassie corrected herself swiftly. 'Professor Merrick's secretary.' She'd felt sorry for the other girl yesterday but she had to admit that her manners could be improved. She glimpsed the grey car waiting in the lane, a young man at the wheel. Boyfriend? 'How can I help you?' she enquired briskly. After the way Adam had reacted to the student yesterday, she very much doubted that he would welcome her unreservedly into his home.

'Professor Merrick promised to lend me a textbook to help with my assignment. I can't get hold of it in the library.'

'I see.' Cassie hesitated, instinctively doubtful of the veracity of the statement. 'If you'd just like to wait a second, I'll check...' As she started to turn away, the taller girl pushed by her into the hall, her entrance coinciding with Adam Merrick's descent down the stairs.

With a drop of her heart Cassie saw the shutters slam over his eyes, the muscles of his strong jaw tauten. No doubt she was going to be blamed for this unwanted intrusion, but what the hell had he expected her to do? Physically bar the other girl from entering the house?

'Susan.' His voice was clipped and terse. 'If you'd like to come into my study for a moment.' He opened the door to his left. 'Thank you, Cassandra.' He glanced back over his shoulder, his expression thunderous.

'You should have answered the bell yourself. I'm not your damn butler,' Cassie hissed ferociously at him. 'Nor your bouncer,' she added, her scowl intensifying as the door was slammed soundly in her face.

Ill-mannered oaf! She moved down the hall. Selfish pig. Would it honestly hurt him to give the student a few minutes of his precious time? The girl was obviously worried sick about that assignment she kept referring to and it must have taken a lot of courage to tackle Adam in his lair after his appalling rudeness yesterday. She wandered into the kitchen, sat down on a stool and then jumped up, stiffening as she heard the sound of noisy, uncontrollable sobbing from the hall.

Darting back out of the kitchen, she saw the student leaning against the hall wall, tears pouring down her cheeks.

'Hey, it can't be that bad.' Eyes dark with compassion, Cassie fished out a clean tissue from the pocket of her jeans and pressed it into the weeping girl's hand. 'Come and have a cup of tea,' she urged gently, shooting a disgusted glance into the study. What on earth had he said to reduce the poor girl to this state?

'He...he doesn't want me in his tutorial group any more. He's going to transfer me to someone else's...' Susan removed her misted glasses and wiped them frantically with the tissue. 'It's so unfair... I'd do anything in the world for him... Give up Roger... I love him so much...'

Oh, God. Cassie winced. Why hadn't she realised from the start that the girl was completely infatuated with her lecturer? As the girl began to sob noisily again, Cassie instinctively put a comforting arm across her shoulder, but recognised that her sympathy was waning, that she was now fighting the temptation to shake the other girl to her senses. Adam Merrick wasn't worth this! She jerked her head up as she saw the figure looming in the study doorway.

'Still here, Susan?' he enquired mildly, his expression completely bland. Oblivious to the sparks in her grey eyes, he smiled down into Cassie's upturned face. 'Did I hear you mention something about tea, sweetheart?' Before she had time to register what was happening, he inclined his head and implanted a light kiss on top of her red curls. 'I'll go and help myself. Can't have you worn to a frazzle running around after me before we're even married,' he murmured considerately and, whistling unconcernedly under his breath, moved down the hall.

'You're engaged to Professor Merrick? How could you lie, pretend you were just his secretary... let me make such a fool of myself...?'

From a long way away, Cassie heard the other girl's raised voice, followed by the crashing of the front door. Then, whipping round, she walked jerkily towards the kitchen.

Adam was by the sink filling up the kettle with his left hand. He didn't look up as she approached but she could see the muscle flickering along the hard line of his jaw, could almost feel the anger emanating from his body. Why the hell was he so angry when...?

'That was an utterly despicable thing to do,' she said contemptuously. 'And next time you want to play infantile games, don't damn well involve me!' Her voice was no longer as controlled as she would have liked; she could hear it beginning to rise. 'That poor girl thinks she's in love with you. You could have been kinder to her, shown some compassion!'

'Don't be so damn naïve!' The blue eyes swept over her. 'How the hell do you think she would have responded if I had been more sympathetic? She'd have taken it as direct encouragement.'

Cassie smiled. 'And would you have been quite so intent on discouraging her if she'd been a little more attractive?' she enquired sweetly. He sounded so arrogant, so damn egoistical, as if he were constantly having to fend off unwanted feminine advances...

'And what the hell is that supposed to mean?' His voice cracked the air like a whip as he took a step towards her.

She flinched from the anger in his eyes, already regretting the snide insinuation that she knew instinctively was unfounded. Professor Adam Merrick would never abuse his position, take advantage of his impressionable female students. But something inside her drove her on.

'Oh, come on, Professor, don't be so naïve,' she taunted. 'Surely you don't want me to spell it out for you? Ouch!' she yelped in protest as a strong hand snaked around her wrist, propelling her forwards.

'Would you let me go, you overgrown bully?' she demanded furiously, her eyes dilating with alarm as she saw the ominous expression on the dark face bending towards her. She could feel his breath on her cheeks, see the chiselled line of his mouth a few inches above her own. Frantically she tried to wrench her arm from the vice-like grip. 'Let me——' The words choked in her throat as the hard mouth came down on hers, bruising her lips, grinding them against her teeth in a merciless onslaught.

Her free hand pushed ineffectually against the solid wall of his chest and fell helplessly to her side. Shockwaves tingled down her spine. She no longer seemed to have the strength or will to struggle. She couldn't breathe, could feel the blood pounding in her ears, her heart hammering against her ribcage. She felt dizzy, disorientated, oblivious to everything but the hard punishing mouth, violating her senses, demanding complete capitulation.

The warmth curdling in the pit of her stomach flared into a furnace, scalding heat teasing through her veins, igniting every nerve-ending in her body. No longer capable of coherent thought, aware only of that searing ache inside her, Cassie's arms locked around Adam's neck. Eyes closed, she arched against him, her lips parting unresistingly beneath the urgent, insistent mouth, tasting him as he was her, drowning in a whirlpool of fierce, escalating, sensual pleasure.

Her hand, no longer commanded by her mind but by some alien force, slid beneath the collar of his shirt, her fingers tingling as they moved slowly over the warm, smooth male skin, revelling in the hard band of muscle beneath her touch. She lost all sense of time; there was nothing but this man and that tormenting, driving need inside her.

As he abruptly lifted his head she felt bereft, confused, the release too sudden. Legs trembling, she focused her dazed eyes on his face.

'Quite the little seductress, hmm? Thanks for the offer, Cassandra, but no, thanks.' The sneering taunting words, the contempt in the harsh grating voice were as effective as a physical blow in shocking her back to reality.

She recoiled backwards, the colour ebbing from her face as she absorbed the implication of his words, saw the disdain and derision in the dark blue eyes.

'H-how d-dare you?' Her breathing was shallow, erratic.

'How dare you?' Adam mimicked caustically. Leaning back against the table, he folded his arms indolently across his deep chest. 'It's a little late for the outraged Victorian miss routine, isn't it? I could take you to bed right now if I chose.' The blue eyes moved slowly and insolently over her body, lingering deliberately on the swelling curve of her rounded breasts. His mouth curled contemptuously. 'Except I don't choose. I prefer my women to be a little more of a challenge, a little more subtle. Not quite so eager and willing.'

'You disgusting——' she was shaking so much she could hardly force the words through her stiff lips '—disgusting, arrogant...'

'Bastard?' he completed derisively. 'If you're as unimaginative in bed as you are in your choice of adjective——'

Her mind blocked to the tormenting words, hardly aware of what she was doing, Cassie raised her hand and struck a stinging blow across the side of his face. Then, spinning on her heel, she marched into the hall.

CHAPTER SIX

LOCKING the door of the downstairs cloakroom behind her, Cassie leant against it and took a deep, ragged breath, willing her shaking legs not to subside beneath her. She'd never in her life struck another human being, had never before felt so close to losing complete control of herself. But then she'd never encountered such a loathsome, despicable... Her hands closed into fists, the nails digging into her palms. She hated him. Hated him with every fibre in her being. 'I could take you to bed right now if I chose...' Oh, God. She pressed her hands to her face, closing her eyes, trying to obliterate the taunting words, the scornful, contemptuous face from her mind.

Adam's kiss had been executed purely out of anger—he might just as easily have released his feelings by shaking her by the scruff of her neck. And she hadn't even tried to resist, had responded with a fierce, wanton abandonment that had not only shocked but terrified her. She must have been insane... how could she...? She groaned out loud. And now he thought she was a pushover.

So what? Her small chin squared resolutely. Who the hell cared what Professor Adam Merrick thought? His opinion was worthless. She was damned if she was going to torture herself with pointless recriminations over what, when all was said and done, had merely been a kiss. And regardless of her response, he had been the one to instigate it. Her eyes sparked. The arrogance, the gall, the unbelievable conceit of the man... How dared he insinuate that if it hadn't been for his disinclination they would have ended up in bed together? Was that how his sordid little mind worked? One kiss... next stop bed...

101

She moved towards the basin and tensed with renewed horror as she caught sight of her reflection in the mirror. Her eyes were over-bright, her lower lip swollen, but it was her body's humiliating betrayal that made her shudder with self-revulsion. Her swollen breasts, the nipples taut and engorged, were thrust uninhibitedly against the soft fabric of her sweatshirt. Her throat constricted. Is that how she'd looked when...? So...so wanton? *Eager. Willing.*

Swallowing hard, she averted her gaze and bending over the white porcelain basin splashed warm water on to her face. She felt physically and emotionally drained, battered inside, couldn't even think straight any more. She just wanted to escape from this house, escape from Adam Merrick, ached for the warm, safe sanctuary of Mead Cottage.

She dabbed her face dry with a towel. The temptation simply to jump in the car and go was overwhelming... No! She refused to take that weak, coward's course. Pride and the restoration of her self-respect demanded that she faced him again. Faced him with a cool, calm indifference. She wouldn't give him the satisfaction of slinking away.

Gritting her teeth, she unlocked the door and tensed as she heard footsteps in the hall, relief swamping her as she identified the two separate treads, the lighter one easily recognisable as William's. She wouldn't have to face Adam on his own.

Taking a deep breath she emerged from the cloakroom.

'Cassie!' William, in the process of removing his school coat, rushed towards her and greeted her with an enthusiastic hug. 'I did this for you today.' Nonchalantly, but with ill-concealed pride, he held up a brightly crayoned picture for her inspection. 'That's me, that's Lisa and that's you and Uncle Adam,' he trebled, pointing with his finger. 'You can keep it if you like,' he added casually.

'Thank you. I'll hang it on my bedroom wall,' she promised, noting wryly how Adam dominated the picture. Schooling her features into impassivity, she flicked him a quick glance over the top of William's head, jolting as she saw the red weal on the side of his face. God, she hadn't realised she'd hit him with quite such force... Well, he'd asked for it. She refused to feel even the slightest qualm of guilt.

'Shall we play football first? And then have tea?' William claimed her attention again, looking up at her eagerly.

'Cassandra won't be staying to tea tonight,' Adam's cool, commanding voice cut in. 'She's just going home.'

Cassie's mouth tightened. She was perfectly capable of answering for herself. He looked back at her, his face devoid of all expression, a blank controlled mask.

'Will you come back later? And say goodnight?'

Her eyes dropped back to the small boy. William, I would if it were at all possible, she thought silently as she gently shook her head. She was startled by the speed with which a bond seemed to be forming between her and William. Or was William just naturally outgoing and friendly, ready to shower his affection on anyone prepared to give him their time and attention?

'Will you be here tomorrow, then?' he persisted.

'It's Saturday tomorrow,' she said evasively, feeling a sudden tearing pang of sadness at the knowledge that she most probably would never see the small boy again. She ruffled the dark head and, turning away, dragged her jacket off the coat peg behind her. As she shrugged it on, Adam strode by her and held the front door open.

'Goodbye, Cassandra.' His eyes were like ice.

She turned away, registering the finality with which he had uttered the word, registering too that instead of the expected relief there was a curious tightness in her chest, and she felt a dull, dreary sense of anticlimax.

* * *

Cassie sat cross-legged on her bed, absently stroking the tortoiseshell cat curled up on her lap as she surveyed the map on her bedroom wall. Still so much of the world left to see. She hadn't even explored her own native country properly yet.

Her eyes moved sideways and fell on the picture William had bestowed upon her yesterday and which she'd faithfully pinned to the wall as promised. Tipping the cat gently from her lap, she unfurled her jean-clad legs and scrambled off the bed. She crossed the cream carpet to the window and gazed out at the sheeting rain. If it weren't for Kate, she would pack her rucksack right this minute and go...

She turned away from the window and padded restlessly around the room. She really ought to start making plans for the future. How long was she going to continue with her nomadic, day-to-day existence? She flopped down on the bed and received an irate glare from the cat as she disturbed its slumber. Perhaps she would consider reapplying to university—not the local one, of course—and maybe aim for a career that involved travel. She would be twenty-three at the start of the next academic year. Would she be classed as a mature student? She grinned. 'Mature' would be the last adjective she'd use to describe herself right now. She felt tetchy, tense, as wound up as a coiled spring ready to snap any moment, and wanted very badly to open the window, stick her head out and scream at the top of her lungs. Exercise, she decided firmly. That was the antidote to this inexplicable mood: a burst of frenetic physical activity to work off all that pent-up explosive energy inside her.

Jumping to her feet, she left the bedroom and went in search of her aunt, discovering her in the kitchen.

'Finished unpacking?' Kate glanced up, breadknife in her hand. 'Cheese sandwich?'

'Mmm. Please.' Cassie sat down on a chair beside the table and cupped her chin in her hands. 'Thought I might go for a swim this afternoon. Fancy coming?'

Kate grinned over her shoulder. 'I was planning to put my feet up and watch a sloppy film on the box.' Her expression altered as she continued to study her niece. 'Are you sure you're feeling better? You still look very pale. I hope you're not coming down with this flu virus.'

'I feel fine,' Cassie said quickly, feeling slightly guilty about the manufactured headache of yesterday evening which she'd used to explain her uncharacteristically subdued mood and desire for an early night. She stiffened as the telephone pealed in the landing.

Sighing, Kate put down the breadknife and disappeared through the hall. Automatically Cassie stood up, rinsed her hands and continued with the sandwich preparations. It was the fourth call of the morning on Kate's private line and each time her heart had skipped an uneasy beat. Adam was bound to call sooner or later to dispense officially with her secretarial services and demand the return of his car which she'd driven home unthinkingly yesterday. Not that he'd made any attempt to stop her. Her eyebrows knitted together over her dark, brooding eyes. She had absolutely no desire to see that arrogant, obnoxious male as long as she lived. So why was she still experiencing that flat, empty sensation that had been with her ever since she'd returned to Mead Cottage?

She placed the sandwiches on two plates and set them on the table, glancing up enquiringly as Kate appeared.

'That was Adam,' she announced casually, sitting down at the table.

Cassie tensed expectantly, her eyes on her plate.

'He's asked me to go to the theatre with him tonight. He did mention it on Thursday but wasn't sure whether he'd manage to get a sitter for William. But apparently William's now been invited to tea and to spend the night with one of his school friends.' Kate paused. 'Would you mind dreadfully if I went . . . ? It's just that it's *The Doll's House* and I do love Ibsen.'

Cassie's head jerked up. 'Of course I don't mind...why ever should I?' As she saw the startled expression on Kate's face, she snapped her mouth shut, battling unsuccessfully to stop the soft wash of colour flooding her cheek. Why had she sounded so absurdly defensive? Kate hadn't been asking if she minded the fact that she was going out with Adam for the evening; she'd merely been concerned that her niece would be left on her own. Uncomfortably aware that Kate was watching her, she took a swift bite of her sandwich, swallowing it without even tasting it. Hadn't he even mentioned her or the car?

'Oh, and I've asked Adam for lunch tomorrow. William, too, of course.' She frowned. 'Is something the matter, Cass?'

Cursing herself for not controlling her expression of utter dismay more quickly, Cassie shook her head and smiled blithely. 'No, of course not.' She avoided looking directly at her aunt. 'Any idea of the swimming pool times?'

'There's a leaflet in the sitting-room somewhere.'

'Thanks. I'll have a look in a moment.' Cassie knew that Kate was aware that she'd deliberately changed the subject but knew too that her aunt wouldn't pursue the matter. Kate had always made time to listen to her, but even when she'd been a child had respected her right to privacy, had never forced an unwilling confidence.

She forced down the remainder of her sandwich, waited until Kate had finished and stood up. 'Think I'll go and root out my costume,' she murmured and, for the first time in her life, felt a sense of relief as she escaped Kate's presence.

It had stopped raining and she elected to walk to the local sports centre, taking an almost perverse pleasure in battling against the stinging cold wind. She pounded up and down the pool until she was exhausted and then went up to the cafeteria and ordered coffee.

What malicious quirk of fate had brought Adam Merrick back into Kate's life again? Why of all the universities in the world had he to take up a post at the local one? She scowled down into her coffee. Life was going to become unbearable if he became a regular visitor to Mead Cottage. The only consolation, she supposed, was that she'd at least be able to stay in contact with William. Her scowl deepened. How could someone as intelligent and discerning as Kate be so blind as not to see straight through Adam's superficial charm? Oh, hell. Tiny goosebumps tingled down her spine and she closed her eyes despairingly. If only she could obliterate the memory of that hard, expert mouth against hers, if only the image of a pair of brilliant, taunting blue eyes set in a dark, mocking face wouldn't keep floating unbidden and unwanted into her head...

'Finished with your cup, love? We're just closing.'

'Er—yes, thanks.' She nodded absently at the middle-aged woman hovering by the table, and with a start realised that she was the sole remaining customer. Rising to her feet, she swung her sports bag over her shoulder.

It was dark as she emerged from the sports centre and she huddled into her coat, turning up the collar against the wind. She contemplated catching a bus and then decided against it, unhappily aware that she was deliberately delaying her inevitable return to Mead Cottage. Kate would be starting to prepare for her evening ahead with Adam soon. Her stomach lurched painfully. Hunger pangs, she informed herself briskly, increasing her pace as she felt the first spot of rain lash against her face.

As she turned into the familiar street, she saw that Kate hadn't pulled the curtains, the light from the upstairs flat sending out an inviting glow into the cold darkness. Fishing out her key, she entered the back door, tugging off her dripping jacket as she climbed the stairs.

'Hi, Kate, I'm home.'

The bathroom door opened and Kate stuck her head around the door. 'Good swim? Oh, Cass, you're drenched.' She tossed a towel towards her.

'Thanks.' Cassie started to rub her hair. 'What time are you picking Adam up?'

'He insisted on getting a taxi over here to save all that backtracking.'

'How very considerate,' Cassie muttered acidly, instantly regretting it as her aunt's forehead creased.

'If he arrives before I'm decent, would you let him in?'

'No, I'll leave him shivering on the doorstep, Auntie,' Cassie answered drily, oddly relieved by Kate's quick responsive grin.

Padding to her bedroom, she tugged off her sodden clothes and dried her hair. She fished out a pair of black denims from her cupboard and then hesitated. Tossing them aside, she moved across to the wardrobe, inspected the meagre contents, pulled out an olive-green woollen dress and slipped it over her head. She inspected herself in the mirror, registering without vanity that the old but favourite dress still suited her, the colour enhancing the rich red-gold of her hair, the deceptive severity of the style perversely emphasising the feminine curves beneath the soft fabric.

Ignoring the enquiring voice that hammered in her head, she sat down at the dressing-table, applied mascara to her thick lashes and carefully outlined the curve of her mouth with pink lip gloss. Picking up the bottle of her favourite scent, she sprayed a discreet amount on her wrists and then froze, staring into the mirror. A girl with wide, confused grey eyes stared back at her in bewilderment. What exactly was she playing at? Come on, you know exactly what you're doing, the voice in her head jeered.

She tensed as the doorbell echoed through the flat, pulled a face in the mirror and stood up. Slipping her feet into a pair of low-heeled evening shoes, she made her way downstairs. An expression of warm welcome on her face, she flung open the door.

'You're early...' she began eagerly and then, as she saw the shadowy figure towering on the threshold, her face dropped.

'Good evening, Cassandra.'

'Oh, it's you,' she muttered, her voice heavy with disappointment. 'I thought...' She broke off. 'Kate's not quite ready.' She shrugged. 'I suppose you'd better come in.' Her sense of smell was teased by the subtle fragrance of aftershave, the minty tang of toothpaste. Turning away quickly, she led him upstairs into the sitting-room.

'You can wait in here,' she informed him brusquely.

'Thank you,' Adam murmured drily. Giving the open log fire an appreciative look, he lowered his powerful frame into a chair, stretching out his dark, tailored leg indolently in front of him. A red silk tie rested against the brilliant white of his shirt.

'Do make yourself at home.' Cassie surveyed him from under her long lashes, irritated beyond measure by his casual, relaxed posture, by the intangible aura of unassailable male assurance that seemed to be invading the whole room. This was the first time he'd ever visited Mead Cottage and he already looked as if he owned the place. The soft light from the standard lamp behind his head cast a shadow over the strong planes of his face, darkened his eyes until they were navy blue. She averted her eyes, moving towards the door.

'If you'll excuse me, I'm in rather a rush,' she said with frigid courtesy, permitting her lips to curve in a small smile of pleasurable anticipation.

'Sit down, Cassandra!'

She paused, her hackles rising instantly in response to the cool, commanding voice. Who the hell did he think he was, issuing orders in this house? She threw him a disdainful glance over her shoulder. 'I'm not on duty now, Professor Merrick.'

'Sit!'

She spun round towards him, eyes glinting. 'I haven't a wet nose, nor a tail!' Then to her chagrin and amazement, she found herself obeying, sinking weakly on to the sofa.

'What happened yesterday was a mistake,' he said crisply and without preamble. 'And one I have no intention of repeating.'

Cassie leant back in her chair and crossed a slim leg over the other one. Was that supposed to be an apology? And what exactly had been the 'mistake'? Kissing her? Or his vile insinuations afterwards? She gave a slow, dulcet smile. 'Scared that I might tell Kate?' she enquired sweetly.

He smiled back at her. 'So what's his name?' he drawled.

'Er?' Cassie grunted inelegantly, caught completely off guard by the unexpected question. Oh, hell. She'd completely forgotten about her fictitious date... She stiffened. She didn't trust that lazy smile, that glint in his eyes.

'Tsk, tsk, Cassandra. Can't even remember his name, hmm?' He laughed softly.

'I hardly think that my personal life is any of your concern,' she said coolly, her hands tightening around the arm of the chair. What on earth had prompted her to engage in the stupid, juvenile subterfuge? she berated herself, squirming inwardly. She was acutely conscious of the blue eyes resting on her averted face, felt every muscle in her body tensing under his mocking gaze as she battled to stop the betraying wash of colour flooding her cheeks. She'd thought she'd cured herself of blushing in her teens—but ever since she'd laid eyes on Adam Merrick, she seemed to have been regressing back towards adolescence, she thought bitterly. It was as if his own indomitable confidence and assurance somehow sapped her own.

'Adam, I'm sorry to have kept you waiting.'

Cassie's gaze jerked to the door as Kate walked into the room, and then darted back to Adam, witnessing the undisguised male appreciation etched on his rugged features as he rose to his feet.

'You look wonderful, Katherine,' he murmured softly, moving towards her. Stooping, he kissed her lightly on the cheek.

He was right, Cassie agreed, ignoring the knot in the pit of her stomach. Kate did look wonderful. The red silk jersey dress, adorned with a simple pearl necklace, was the perfect foil for her dark hair and eyes. She looked poised and elegant . . . in fact the ideal companion for the tall, lean man with the intelligent, compelling face. Her throat went dry.

'See you later, Cass.'

'Have a good time.' Cassie beamed back at her aunt. She heard the rumble of Adam's voice, followed by Kate's light responsive laugh as their footsteps receded down the landing. Jumping to her feet, she switched on the television and threw herself down on the sofa staring mindlessly at the images flickering across the screen.

He hadn't even given her the most cursory of glances once Kate had entered the room, hadn't even had the courtesy to bid her good night, had forgotten her existence completely.

At first she thought the sharp ringing tone was issuing from the television and then, as if waking from a trance, realised that it was the telephone. Reluctantly she rose to her feet and went to answer it.

'Hello, Freckles.'

'Richard!' She recognised his voice straight away. 'How are you? I thought you were coming down with this flu virus.' He might infuriate her at times with his over-casual attitude towards her aunt, but she was still genuinely fond of Richard, whom Kate had first met when, as a newly qualified solicitor, he had handled the purchase of Mead Cottage. Over the ensuing years he had proved himself to be a staunch and reliable friend to both of them.

'Turned out just to be a head cold. So how's everything with you?'

They chatted casually for a few moments and then inevitably Richard asked to speak to Kate.

'I'm afraid she's not here.'

'Surely she's not working on a Saturday night?'

Cassie's eyes rested thoughtfully on the phone. Did Richard believe that Kate had no social life of her own at all? That unless she was working she spent every evening in the flat hoping for a call from him? Why was the male of the species so appallingly damn arrogant?

'Actually she's gone to the theatre.' She hesitated for a second. What the hell? 'With Adam Merrick.' If Richard honestly regarded Kate as nothing more than a friend, then he shouldn't object to her seeing another man. And if he found that the news did trouble him, then maybe that was just the jolt he needed to shake his complacency.

There was a long silence at the other end of the line and Cassie would have given anything to be able to see Richard's expression.

'Oh, I see,' he said finally. He cleared his throat. 'Um, is she very keen on this Merrick chap?'

Cassie's lips twitched. Aha. A touch of the old green-eyed monster? Unconsciously she traced a pattern in the carpet with her foot. She didn't really have a clue about Kate's feelings towards Adam. Perhaps her aunt didn't know herself. After all, he'd only come back into her life a couple of days ago... 'Yes.' She heard a voice she couldn't believe her own saying positively. 'She is. Very.'

There was another pause. 'And how about him? Does he feel the same? I mean, I'm just concerned about Kate. I wouldn't want her to get hurt...'

Really, Richard? Her eyes darkened as she reviewed his question. Adam's air of complete well-being yesterday morning after he'd met Kate again, the look in his eyes tonight. Her heart gave an unexpected squeeze. 'Yes,' she said quietly, forcing the affirmative out through suddenly dry lips, 'he does.' She ought not to be discussing Kate like this... She took a deep breath. 'If you're not careful, Richard, you're going to lose her,' she said in a quick rush, and before he had time to respond put the receiver down.

Aghast, she walked slowly back into the sitting-room and sat down on the sofa, staring rigidly ahead. She'd absolutely no right to interfere in Kate's personal life.

Oh, what the heck! She squared her small chin defiantly. She'd only had Kate's best interests at heart, and it was about time someone stirred Richard up, made him stop taking her for granted.

Oh, come off it, Cassandra. Who are you trying to kid? She hadn't been acting purely out of altruism; she desperately wanted Richard to intervene before her aunt's relationship with Adam developed any further. Admit it, she ordered herself harshly, the colour draining from her face. You're jealous.

She was jealous of the person she loved most in the world and to whom she owed a debt that could never be paid, jealous because that person was spending the evening with a man she herself had only met three days ago. A man, moreover, who'd made it quite clear he despised her. It was all so ludicrous she ought to be laughing...

It wasn't as if she even liked Adam Merrick, she told herself fiercely. He hadn't invaded her heart or her mind. No, it was far more basic than that, she thought with burning self-disgust. Physical attraction. Humiliatingly and degradingly simple. She clenched her teeth together. How could she be so weak, so shallow as to allow her response to a man to be governed not by reason or emotion, but solely by the dictates of her hormones?

Her throat constricted, her stomach muscles cramping into tortuous knots. The thought of Adam smiling down at Kate, holding her, kissing her... Appalled and

ashamed by her mental voyeurism, she jumped to her
feet, paced around the room with jerky strides. Coming
to a halt, she took a deep, controlling breath.

Whatever happened she mustn't do anything to alert
Kate's suspicions, do anything to mar her relationship
with Adam. Years ago she'd innocently been the cause
of Kate's break-up with Andrew Merrick; fate had now
brought the twin brother of the man Kate had once loved
back into her life. And this time, Cassie thought resolutely, she wasn't going to be responsible for jeopard-
ising her aunt's potential happiness in any way.

She suddenly caught sight of her white, tense face in
the mirror over the mantelpiece and began to grin. Very
noble, Cassandra, she mocked herself, but aren't you
jumping the gun a bit? Kate was only going to the theatre
with Adam, for Pete's sake, not riding off into the sunset
on his white charger...

Cassie glanced up from the floor where she was playing
a complicated game with William, involving marbles, a
stick and an assortment of toy cars, the rules of which
were completely beyond her comprehension. Kate and
Adam were sitting on the settee, a coffee tray set on the
table in front of them.

'Your turn,' William announced.

'Right.' Hoping she was making a wise move, Cassie
picked up the stick and used it to nudge a marble towards
a miniature lorry.

'I don't think you really understand this properly.'
William shook his head reprovingly. 'P'raps we'd better
play something easier.'

'Yes,' Cassie agreed humbly. It would probably help
if she concentrated more, but her attention kept
wandering.

William collected up the marbles and cars, stowed
them in the canvas bag he'd brought with him and extracted a draughts-board. He'd evidently taken it upon
himself to entertain her for the afternoon, she thought

with amusement. Her eyes flickered back to the settee. Adam's arm was stretched along the back, his hand almost but not quite touching Kate's shoulder. She looked away quickly.

Since greeting her when he arrived, Adam had barely exchanged two words with her and then it had been with the indifferent courtesy he would have accorded a stranger. During lunch he'd concentrated his attention on Kate; Cassie in turn had been monopolised by William, and had studiously avoided even glancing across at Adam. The meal itself, a traditional roast, had, judging by the appreciative murmurs, been excellent, although she herself had barely tasted it.

The tortoiseshell cat sauntered into the room and, with feline perverseness, settled down in the middle of the draughts-board and, much to William's delight, began to nudge the black and white counters with a delicate paw.

'Back in a minute,' Cassie murmured, scrambling to her feet. The small boy nodded without looking up, his whole attention focused on his new-found friend. She walked across the carpet and then paused in the doorway, glancing back over her shoulder. Her eyes moved slowly over the three dark heads and her heart constricted. They looked like the perfect family unit. Adam and Kate weren't talking, but their silence was one of easy familiarity, indicative of the bond that would always exist between them, a bond of shared experiences and past memories. Suddenly she felt completely shut out, cold, isolated, empty...

Swallowing the lump in her throat, she made her way along the hall to the kitchen. Kate had been disappointingly reticent at breakfast about the previous night. She'd evidently enjoyed the theatre production but had hardly mentioned Adam at all.

Cassie had studied her aunt discreetly. Did she look starry-eyed, deliriously happy, like a woman on the brink of falling madly in love? It had been difficult to reach any conclusion with Kate sitting there reading the Sunday newspapers, clad in a dressing-gown with a towel wrapped around her recently-washed hair.

Retrieving the bread bin, Cassie extracted the stale crusts she'd been saving and placed them in a plastic bag. What must it be like to be head over heels in love with a man? To be completely dependent on another human being for your own personal happiness? She shuddered, a cold shiver tingling down her spine, her eyes darkening.

Darting into her bedroom, she tugged off her pink sweatshirt and replaced it with her old navy blue Guernsey. She glanced swiftly in the mirror, ran a hand through her tumbled red curls and then, picking up her windproof jacket, made her way back down the landing.

She opened the sitting-room door, momentarily non-plussed at the sight of the stocky, fair-haired man sitting in an armchair by the fire. She hadn't heard the doorbell.

'Hello, Richard.'

He rose to his feet and kissed her lightly on the cheek. 'You look well, Freckles. I like the short hair.'

'Thanks.' The use of the childhood pet name suddenly irritated her, made her feel about six.

'So how long are you home for this time?' Richard continued, sitting down again, smiling up at Kate as she handed him a cup of coffee.

Cassie shrugged. 'Not sure.' She felt a sneaking sympathy for Richard. Despite his broad grin and air of good-humour, he was distinctly ill at ease. He'd doubtless expected to find Kate on her own this afternoon, and it must have been disconcerting to say the least to discover Adam ensconced in the sitting-room. His eyes kept sliding to the sofa, sizing up the other man, clearly resenting his presence. Duelling pistols at dawn? She compressed her lips together to stop the burst of inane laughter that threatened to burst from her.

'Knowing you, you'll have itchy feet by the time Christmas is over.'

'Perhaps,' she said vaguely. She tensed, sensing Adam's eyes on her, and flicked him a cautious glance under her lashes, jolting as she witnessed the forbidding expression on his granite face. What the hell did he have to look so disapproving about? For a brief, almost inperceptible second his eyes met and held hers and then she dropped her gaze, deliberately turning her attention to William who was still sprawled on the carpet with the cat.

'Would you like to go over to the river and feed the ducks?'

He nodded enthusiastically and leapt to his feet. 'I'll go and get my coat.'

'You'll need wellingtons too,' Cassie advised, having spotted the small pair of boots sticking out of the canvas bag. William had evidently come prepared for every contingency.

'See you later,' she murmured to the room at large, moving towards the door.

'I'll come with you.'

Cassie stiffened with surprise and dismay as she heard the deep, casual drawl and, turning round, saw Adam rising leisurely to his feet. He was so arrogantly sure of himself. It would never occur to him that she didn't want his company. Neither apparently did he feel in the least bit threatened by Richard's presence, had no qualms about leaving Kate alone with him.

'It'll be very muddy by the river after all the rain yesterday,' she said coldly, her eyes dropping pointedly to Adam's well-polished Italian shoes.

'I always keep a pair of wellingtons in the back of the car,' he returned easily. He quirked a dark eyebrow. 'Keys?'

Shrugging, Cassie fetched the stale bread and car keys from the kitchen and herded William down the stairs and out of the back door.

Once Adam had donned his boots and waxed jacket, she led him and William to the end of the walled garden

and out through the wooden gate that gave direct access
on to the river tow-path.

'The ducks are usually a bit further down, just round
the bend,' she told William. 'Be careful you don't slip
over,' she called after him as she scampered ahead,
startling two coots who scuttled frantically to the safety
of the reeds on the opposite bank.

'I won't,' he assured her, splashing joyously through
a muddy puddle.

Cassie usually loved sauntering by the river, relished
the tranquillity and peace. It was a place to think, to
dream. But today the magic didn't seem to be working.
It wasn't William distracting her, but the man striding
silently by her side. She was too aware of him, couldn't
seem to shut herself off from his presence and yet, at
the same time, she felt completely isolated from him.
She flicked him a quick glance, eyes moving swiftly over
the uncompromisingly male features. His expression was
masked, gave absolutely no indication as to his thoughts.
It would take a lifetime to understand this man, to be
able to gauge his moods and feelings, to comprehend
what was actually going on in that dark head. With
sudden ferocity she kicked a small pebble.

William had come to a standstill, watching a man on
the far bank throwing a stick for his Labrador dog.

'Why haven't you got a dog?' he asked Cassie curiously. 'Don't you like them?'

'Yes, I do.' Cassie smiled, her tension easing as she
looked down into the small face.

'Why don't you get one, then?' Not waiting for an
answer, he raced on down the path.

Perhaps she would get a dog one day, Cassie mused.
One day. There were so many things she was going to
do when that far-off day arrived. Finally take up her
place at university. Choose a career. Settle down...

'Dogs are a commitment. A tie.'

Cassie's eyes jerked to the dark face as the cold, caustic
voice interrupted her thoughts.

'And what is that meant to mean?' she enquired frigidly. What did he think she was going to do—rush out and buy a puppy on a whim and abandon it a few days later?

'I was just pointing out the obvious,' he said coolly. 'Animals, like children, aren't something you can just pet for a few minutes when the mood suits you and put back in the cupboard. They require long-term commitment.' His eyes were like blocks of ice. 'That's something you've been running away from all your life, isn't it, Cassie?'

'Commitment to what?' she flung back. 'A career? A man? Just because I've chosen not to join the rat-race or settle down and play happy families . . .' Oh, why was she even bothering? This man could think what the hell he liked about her. And why had he bothered to accompany her if his sole aim had been to bait her?

She turned away and everything fled from her mind as she saw the expression of delight on William's face as he caught his first glimpse of the ducks.

'Be careful,' she called out with sudden alarm as he moved to the edge of the riverbank, acutely conscious of the deep, dark water just below him. One slip . . . She darted towards him, but Adam was already there, holding William's hand firmly in his.

'Here you are.' She handed over the bag of bread and then took a step backwards. Unobserved she stood motionless, watching the small boy with the tall, protective man by his side entice the ducks towards the bank. She swallowed to alleviate the tautness in her throat. There was a deep yearning ache inside her that was almost like a physical pain in its intensity.

'Don't you want to feed them too?' William turned round, holding out a crust of bread.

Cassie smiled, took a step forward, tripped over a tuft of grass and went hurtling towards the river. The next second her legs were lifted from beneath her and she was lying on her back, winded, in a pool of dank, muddy water.

'What a tackle, Uncle Adam!'

Gasping for breath, she eased herself gingerly into a sitting position. William was staring up at his uncle, his face aglow with hero-worship. 'You didn't hurt your wrist again?' he added anxiously.

'No.' Adam ruffled the small dark head.

Blast his wrist! What about her? Cassie gazed at them both in disbelief. She could be lying on the ground unconscious for all the notice they were taking! Glowering, she scrambled to her feet.

'All right?' Adam glanced at her casually as she stalked towards them.

So he'd finally remembered her existence. 'No, I'm not all right,' she snapped. Vainly she tried to wipe some of the damp, sticky mud from her clothes and simply succeeded in transferring it to her hands and face. She felt wet, cold and miserable and it didn't help to have William and Adam standing there eyeing her as if she were something that had just crawled out from a hole. 'You could have knocked me senseless, you great oaf.'

She'd been in no real danger of tumbling into the river, and besides, a restraining hand would have sufficed. She wasn't a damn rugby ball.

'Delayed shock,' Adam murmured mildly to William, who nodded wisely in agreement. His face lit up.

'Your hand's bleeding,' he pointed out with ill-concealed relish.

'Is it?' Little ghoul.

Adam moved towards her. 'Let me see.'

As she felt the firm strong fingers close around her wrist, she flinched, snatching her hand away before he could examine it. 'It's just a graze,' she said shortly.

He towered over her, his eyes dark and unreadable. 'You're shivering,' he said quietly, his hand moving to the zip of his jacket.

Her mouth compressed in a mutinous line, her eyes glinting rebelliously. She didn't want his flipping jacket. Didn't want anything from this man. But with William standing there an interested spectator she had no alternative but to acquiesce.

She recoiled from his touch as he placed the jacket around her shoulders, backing away from him, every instinct urging her to sling the coat back at him. 'Thanks,' she muttered through clenched teeth, and swung away abruptly.

Adam set a brisk pace as they retraced their steps along the path, William at times having to jog-trot to keep up. It was growing dusk, the low river mist beginning to creep over the meadows, turning the ponies that grazed on the far bank into silver phantoms.

'They look as if they haven't any legs,' William observed with fascination, unselfconsciously slipping his hand into Cassie's.

'Mmm.' Cassie smiled down at him. He'd chattered non-stop on the way home, seemingly oblivious of the tension between the two adults. Or was it just she who felt so constrained and edgy? She must look utterly ridiculous, dwarfed in Adam's coat, her face smeared with mud. The grin on Kate's face as she opened the back door confirmed it.

'Sorry, I forgot to take a key.' She kicked off her wellingtons. Richard's car had vanished, so presumably he had gone home.

'What have you been up to?' her aunt enquired, and Cassie saw her exchange smiles with Adam. It made her feel like a recalcitrant child, guilty of playing mud pies in her best party frock. Hell, what had happened to her sense of humour? Why was she being so damn touchy? She squatted down on her haunches and tugged off William's boots.

'You'll stay for tea, Adam?' Kate murmured.

He glanced at his watch. 'Actually, Kate, I think it's time we made a move, thanks all the same.' He turned to William. 'Go up and collect up all your toys, there's a good chap.'

William obediently sped off to the sitting-room while Kate disappeared in search of her car keys. Acutely conscious of the abrupt silence that had fallen, Cassie began to unzip Adam's jacket, cursing silently as it jammed halfway. Her fingers, still numb from cold, struggled unsuccessfully to release it.

'Here. Let me.'

She jumped like a scalded cat as his hand brushed hers, backing away. 'I can manage!'

'Cut it out, Cassandra!' His voice cracked the air like a whip.

Her eyes jerked to his face. His eyebrows were drawn in a thunderous black line, a muscle flickering along the length of the hard, square jaw. 'I d-don't know what you mean.' She'd never seen him look so angry.

'You know damn well what I mean. The terrified virgin routine!' Eyes raking her face, he moved purposefully towards her. 'There you go again!' he grated as she took an involuntary step backwards. 'One meaningless kiss which you weren't exactly averse to, and now I've been cast in the role of potential rapist? Is that it?' His mouth tightened ominously. 'Get one thing straight. The only relationship I'm interested in with you is a working one. And even that, I can assure you, is out of necessity and not...' He broke off, swinging away as William thundered down the stairs towards them, followed more sedately by Kate.

'Ready, Will?' He smiled easily down at his nephew, all traces of anger eradicated from his face.

How could he just switch on and off like that? Cassie wondered in disbelief. He looked as unperturbed, relaxed, as if they'd spent the last few minutes discussing the weather. Her shaking fingers tackled the errant zip again, this time with more success. Shrugging off the coat with relief, she handed it to Adam.

He slung it over a broad shoulder. 'See you tomorrow, Cassie,' he drawled. The blue eyes challenged her wordlessly, and swinging away he followed Kate outside.

'Bye, Cass.' William launched himself towards her, hugging her unceremoniously around the waist.

'You'll get mud all over you,' Cassie murmured gently, her eyes softening as they followed the small figure out of the door.

She was really getting much too fond of William, she mused some time later, as she lay soaking in a hot scented bath. But then why shouldn't she? Surely the more people who loved a child, the better? And even when her temporary employment with Adam was over, she was still sure to see a lot of William because of Kate.

Her mouth tightened, anger twisting through her like a knife, the bar of soap in her hand slipping into the water. God, he was disgusting, despicable. The resolve she'd made not even to think about him vanished. The terrified virgin routine! If only he knew just how apposite that gibe had been ... Nausea gripped her stomach, icy fingers trailing down her spine. She was terrified, she thought bleakly. But not of him ... of herself.

'Cass?'

From a long way away she heard the sound of Kate's voice, realised her aunt was knocking softly at the bathroom door. She had been quick driving Adam and William home, must have come straight back the moment she dropped them off.

'Will you be long? I've something to tell you.'

Quickly Cassie stepped out of the bath and wrapped a towel around her, intrigued by the uncharacteristic excitement in her aunt's voice. She flung open the door, her curiosity intensifying as she saw Kate's glowing eyes and flushed face.

'Tell me,' she implored.

'Oh, Cass, he's asked me to marry him!'

CHAPTER SEVEN

CASSIE stared at her aunt with stunned eyes. She felt sick, her stomach heaving as if she were on a roller-coaster.

'What's the matter? Aren't you pleased?' Kate's happy smile was replaced by a puzzled frown.

Summoning every ounce of willpower, Cassie forced her frozen lips into a grin, but she couldn't meet Kate's eyes. 'Of course I am. I think it's wonderful.' Did the enthusiasm in her voice sound as false to Kate as it did to her own ears? 'I was just so surprised.' She hadn't been prepared for this. Not yet. She just couldn't believe that Kate would rush into something so quickly, marry a man she'd seen three times after a gap of over a decade. 'When did he...? Have you set a date...? What about the agency...?' She couldn't stop rambling. When on earth had Adam actually proposed? Last night? Had Kate been hugging the secret to herself all day?

'I'm dripping water everywhere... I'd better get dressed.' Without giving Kate a chance to say a word, she closed the bathroom door. She just wanted to creep into her bedroom, crawl into bed and pull the covers over her head.

A wave of self-loathing swept over her. Think of Kate, she urged herself. Stop being so damned selfish. Don't spoil her happiness. It seemed to take every ounce of energy to dry herself, tug on her jeans and a dark green jumper. Taking a deep breath, she opened the bathroom door.

Kate was in the hall, murmuring into the telephone. She put down the receiver and turned round. 'That was Richard's mother. He's just told her the news and she's invited us round this evening for a family celebration.'

124

'Richard? You're going to marry Richard?' How could she have been so dense, so stupid? 'He asked you this afternoon? Oh, Kate, it's the most fantastic news in the world. I'm so happy.'

'But I told you... Who else did you think...?' Kate was staring at her in complete mystification. 'Oh, Cass, you didn't think...'

'It's only just sunk in, that's all,' Cassie burbled swiftly and, flinging her arms around her aunt, hugged her. 'After all these years and he's finally proposed!'

'Apparently someone gave him the idea that I was on the verge of some torrid affair with Adam Merrick,' Kate said drily, 'and he discovered that he was jealous.'

'Good heavens,' Cassie murmured wide-eyed, and burst into laughter.

Cassie pulled a sheet of paper from the typewriter and stretched her hands wearily above her head. William would be home from school soon. It would be nice actually to hear the sound of another human voice, she mused acidly, her eyes flicking across to the man behind the oak table. He hadn't said one word to her all afternoon. Unless she counted that grunt when she'd placed a pile of completed correspondence in front of him.

So what was new? Adam had barely spoken to her all week, only addressing her when strictly necessary and then with a brusqueness that at times bordered on downright rudeness. Her eyes moved to the dark head. She was beginning to dread coming to work each morning, beginning to dread seeing Adam's cold, unresponsive face when she arrived. It was only the time she spent with William each afternoon when he returned home from school which made the day bearable.

Despite the physical proximity in which they spent the day, most of the time Adam seemed completely oblivious of her existence. On the occasions she'd been forced to ask him a question, he'd lifted blank eyes and surveyed her in complete silence for a second before answering, as if he were having difficulty in recollecting even who she was. And then when he did remember, his expression indicated that he regretted the necessity which forced him to endure her temporary presence in his home.

She could never relax, was, unfairly, constantly aware of his indomitable, taciturn male presence. Her workload was hardly overtaxing, yet she'd returned to Mead Cottage the last few evenings mentally and physically drained, exhausted by the day's expenditure of nervous energy. But, tired as she was, she was finding it difficult to sleep at night, falling into a fitful doze just before dawn to be woken a short time later by the insistent clamour of the alarm clock.

There was a sharp tap at the door and Mrs Thomas marched in bearing a tray. Placing a mug of tea perfunctorily in front of Cassie, she moved across to Adam's table.

'Thank you, Emily.' He gave her a slow, lazy smile and the tiny woman beamed back down at him.

What a disappointment the temporary housekeeper had proved to be, Cassie mused sourly. A couple of smiles and she was now eating out of Adam's hand.

'I've made another of my special fruit cakes you're so partial to.'

'You're a treasure.'

Oh, yuk. Fetch me a bowl quickly, someone. Cassie's mouth curled disdainfully. Mrs Thomas was practically bridling under the full force of the brilliant blue eyes. How could she be so gullible, not see beyond the superficial charm? A charm, she mused sourly, that Adam never found it necessary to exert on his mere temporary secretary.

'I shan't be in tomorrow or over the weekend, and Annie should be better by Monday, so...'

Adam rose to his feet and handed her a sealed envelope. 'Thank you for everything,' he murmured, escorting her across the room to the door.

Cassie bent her head quickly back over the typewriter, flicking him a quick surreptitious glance as he returned to his desk. She had no idea of what he was working on at the moment. He seemed to spend most of the day reading, pausing from time to time to make notes on a pad by his side. His wrist was improving by the day and he seemed to be experiencing no difficulty in using a pen; presumably it wouldn't be long before he could drive his car again.

She stared out of the window into the bleak, dark afternoon. It would soon be the shortest day, then Christmas. Her eyes glazed over. Where was Adam proposing to spend the festive season? Here at the cottage? Or at the family home? She knew so little about him. She'd been tempted to quiz Kate more about his background, his early life, but had resisted. Not that she'd had much opportunity for doing so, anyway. She'd hardly seen Kate on her own all this past week. Richard was beginning to become a permanent fixture at Mead Cottage.

Her eyes dropped to her desk. Did Adam's grim aloofness have something to do with Kate's engagement? It was a question she'd asked herself repeatedly over the last few days. Kate might regard Adam purely as an old friend, but were his feelings towards her just as platonic or had he hoped for a deeper relationship? Yet when she'd actually told Adam about Kate on Monday, he'd seemed genuinely pleased, had telephoned her immediately to congratulate her. She sighed. Why did she spend so much time trying to analyse him? What was the point?

Gathering up the sheets of paper scattered around the desk, she placed them in a folder and pulled the dustcover over her typewriter. Pushing back her chair, she stood up and began to walk silently across the carpet towards the door.

'Half-day, Cassandra?'

She frowned and turned round. 'Pardon?' she enquired frigidly.

'I employ you from nine to five-thirty.' He glanced at his wristwatch. 'It is now a quarter to four. Added to which, you've spent the last ten minutes staring out of the window in a trance.'

So he'd actually been watching her, had he? The knowledge gave her an uneasy jolt. 'But William will be home any moment...' she began. He would come bursting through the back door starving hungry, expecting to find her in the kitchen waiting for him with a glass of milk and a slice of Mrs Thomas's home-made cake. She wanted to find out how the dress rehearsal for the nativity play had gone, see how he'd fared in his spelling test. 'And I promised to hear him read,' she remembered, unconsciously voicing her thoughts out loud.

'You had no right to make such a promise.'

Cassie's eyebrows drew together. His face looked as if it had been hewn out of ice.

'The agency isn't charging you for the time I spend with William,' she said disdainfully. Is that what was bothering him?

'That is hardly the issue,' he rasped. 'Your temporary function in this house is that of secretary. Nothing more.'

Her function? He was talking about her as if she were a machine...

'And certainly not that of William's nanny,' he continued tersely. 'So would you kindly remember in future that William is not your concern.' A muscle flickered along the line of the square jaw. 'He's not a toy, dammit. You can't simply put him back in the cupboard when you get bored with him.'

Cassie stared at him in disbelief. The man was mad. Stark raving bonkers. Did he honestly think that was how she viewed William? As nothing more than a temporary diversion? She wasn't going to get angry, she or-

dered herself, because that would be acknowledging just
how much his remark had hurt her.

'And instead of standing there wasting even more time,
I suggest you carry on typing out those lecture notes.'
He rose to his feet and began to stride towards the door.

Don't say it, she warned herself quickly. Don't even
hint at what he could do with his lecture notes. She
moved back to her table and sat down. Why was she
even obeying him? she wondered incredulously. Why
didn't she simply down-tools and go?

The gall of the man! Virtually warning her to keep
away from William as if she were some sort of cor-
rupting influence on him. Surely he could see just how
fond she was of his nephew? It was so utterly ludicrous.
Savagely she began to pound the keyboard.

On the dot of five-thirty, she stopped working. She
tidied up her desk and carried the typed lecture notes
across to the oak table. Her eyes dropped to the notepad
over which Adam had been poring all afternoon, and
she raised her eyebrows. It was covered in doodles.
Unable to resist, she flipped back over the pages and
found them similarly inscribed. Tut, tut, Professor.
Hardly a productive afternoon's work. In fact lesser
mortals might be accused of daydreaming, although
doubtless in Adam Merrick's case he'd merely been
having deep, profound thoughts. What had he been
thinking about? Who cared?

She left the room, retrieved her jacket from the hall
and paused, listening to the sound of the firm footsteps
overhead. She began to walk to the front door and
stopped, swinging back round, her eyes darkening resolutely. Adam Merrick could rant and rave all he liked
but she wasn't going meekly home without even saying
goodbye to William.

Chin raised defiantly, she walked swiftly back down
the hall and pushed open the sitting-room door, her eyebrows furrowing as she saw the small boy lying on the
sofa by the fire, a blanket tossed over him.

'Hello, Will.' She smiled down at him, absorbing his heavy eyes and flushed cheeks with mounting concern.

'Hello.' He turned his head listlessly towards her but didn't raise it from the cushion. 'Uncle Adam said you were busy and I wasn't to disturb you.'

'Did he?' she murmured lightly, sitting down on the edge of the sofa. Very gently she laid a hand on his forehead. 'Don't you feel very well?'

Wordlessly he stretched up his arms towards her and Cassie gathered him on to her lap, rocking him slowly backwards and forwards, stroking his hair soothingly. His eyelids began to flicker downwards and very gently she extracted the thumb from his mouth.

She sensed rather than heard Adam enter the room, and raised her head. She met the icy gaze without flinching and then carefully laid the sleeping child back on the sofa, covering him with the rug.

Rising to her feet, she crossed the carpet without looking at Adam and waited in the hall for him to join her.

'Have you called a doctor?' she asked quietly the moment he emerged from the sitting-room, closing the door behind him.

'This is none of your concern.' Arms folded across his chest, he looked down at her, his mouth set in a hard, uncompromising line.

Cassie swallowed back the rising frustration and curdling anger. It wasn't going to help matters to have a slanging match with Adam. If only she could even begin to understand what this was all about, why he had today, out of the blue, suddenly decided to take exception to her interest in William. 'He's obviously coming down with this flu virus,' she said evenly.

'Really?' The dark eyebrows rose sardonically. 'How perceptive of you.'

'Flu isn't a joke,' she snapped, her composure beginning to crack. 'Especially for the young or elderly.

And if you can't be bothered to call the doctor, then I will.' Challenging him with her eyes, she turned away.

'You'll do no such thing!' He caught hold of her wrist and swung her back towards him. 'William's welfare is none of your damn business. Just get that into your head once and for all.' His fingers dug painfully into her bare flesh.

'Will you let me go?' she said steadily. It was he who needed a doctor. A psychiatrist. One who specialised in dealing with unbalanced professors. 'You're hurting me.'

He loosened his grip but didn't release her arm immediately. Eyebrows drawn together, he looked at the livid red blotch on her wrist. His eyes were dark, shadowed, as they looked into hers. 'I'm sorry.'

She looked back at him disdainfully, refusing even to acknowledge his apology. What did he expect her to say anyway? That's quite all right, Professor. Feel free to manhandle me any time you like. After all, I'm only a machine. Besides, it wasn't her wrist that ached, felt raw and bruised. She started to turn away.

'William is becoming very attached to you.'

She paused, startled. So this was what it was all about... 'Don't you think I'm aware of that?' she said quietly.

'Are you?' he enquired brusquely. 'Are you also aware of the responsibility that entails?'

'You think that my feelings for him are just transitory, that——!'

'Your whole life is transitory,' he cut in curtly.

Cassie's eyes sparked. She was trying to have a rational conversation with this man but it was impossible. All he ever did was to make cheap jibes about her lifestyle. 'I care a great deal about William,' she said slowly. 'And when I stop working here, I would like to go on seeing him,' she said evenly.

'Really? And let him grow even more attached to you?' His mouth curled. 'And then what? Abruptly disappear

from his life? A few postcards... Have you any idea of
how vulnerable William still is?'

Something snapped inside her. She of all people could
appreciate that, could empathise totally with William
over the loss of his parents. 'And have you any idea of
why William has become so attached to me? Because I
listen to him when he wants to talk about his mother.
Because you haven't the sensitivity even to understand
that need. Because you still haven't forgiven Rowena for
having the good sense to reject you in favour of your
brother.'

Appalled, she snapped her mouth shut, could have
bitten off her tongue as she saw the raw, naked emotion
on his face, the tearing pain in his eyes. Whatever the
provocation, she'd gone too far. Taunting him about a
woman who was dead. She felt sick with shame.

She ran a tongue over her dry lips. 'Adam?' she said
tentatively. His face was now a cold, dismissive mask.
Oh, what was the use? Defeatedly she walked out of the
front door.

She was in the driveway, in the process of unlocking
Adam's car, when she saw the white saloon draw up in
the lane outside the cottage. A brisk-looking grey-haired
man, with a black bag grasped firmly in one hand,
climbed out and walked purposefully up to the front
door.

Cassie clambered into the car and sat motionlessly in
the driver's seat, gazing unseeingly out of the window.
Why hadn't Adam simply told her that he'd already
called the doctor? That whole unpleasant scene in the
hall could have been avoided completely.

All he'd had to do was to give a civil answer to her
question, a question that had been prompted purely out
of concern for William. There had been no need for
Adam to be so hostile, to lash out at her in the way he
had...

She switched on the ignition and moved down the
drive, slamming on the brakes as she rounded a bend

and saw the dark, bovine shapes illuminated in the headlights. Slumping back in her seat, she watched a muffled figure herd the cows into the farmyard on the left.

He genuinely believed that her interest in William was nothing more than a passing whim. How could he think so little of her, believe her to be so shallow and insensitive? She thumped the steering-wheel with the open palm of her hand. She wished she'd never laid eyes on Adam Merrick, she thought vehemently, moving on cautiously down the lane as the last cow ambled through the farm gate.

She hated the way he seemed to be dominating her every waking thought, infiltrating her dreams, governing her actions. She loathed the knowledge that despite her protestations to the contrary she did care what he thought about her; that he had the ability to hurt her. She wanted him to like her, to respect her, wanted to see his eyes darken with warmth and pleasure when he saw her each morning. Wanted... She didn't know what she wanted. Just wanted that tortuous knot inside her to unwind, set her free of its constraints, wanted that aching, gnawing emptiness inside her to go away. Wanted to be the happy, carefree girl she had been less than two weeks ago.

And that was a junction she had just driven across without even stopping... She expelled a long, shaky breath, her hands suddenly clammy. There could have been a lorry hurtling along the main road... Drawing into the side of the road, she ground to a halt and covered her face with her hands.

Locking the car door behind her, Cassie breathed in the crisp morning air and smiled up at the azure sky overhead. It was impossible to feel downhearted on such a glorious day.

She grinned self-consciously as she walked round to the back of the cottage. She didn't know what had possessed her to get into such a melodramatic tizz last night, working herself into a blinding panic about a mere male.

She shrugged carelessly. OK, she wasn't as immune to Adam Merrick as she would have preferred, but she'd already accepted that. It was nothing she couldn't handle, she told herself with brisk confidence. And neither was she going to give in over William without a fight.

Taking a deep breath, she pushed open the back door and entered the kitchen. 'Morning, Adam.'

He was standing by the stove, stirring the contents of a saucepan. Dark stubble covered his jaw, his thick hair sprang from his head in dishevelled, unruly waves, and he looked as if he had slept in his crumpled navy shirt and jeans. No. He didn't look as if he had slept at all, Cassie amended, her eyes flicking back to his drawn face.

'How's William?' she asked neutrally, concealing her anxiety as she removed her jacket and tossed it absently over a chair.

'He's just woken up.' Adam walked across to the fridge, extracted a bottle of fresh orange juice, poured a quantity into a tumbler and set it on a tray. For the first time Cassie noticed the tiny beads of perspiration on his forehead, the fullness in the usually brilliant blue eyes, the unnatural lethargy in his normal quick, fluid movements. 'Would you take up his breakfast while I have a quick shower? The porridge is almost ready.'

'Of course,' she said quickly. This was hardly the time to get on her high horse, to remind him of yesterday's tirade. 'You ought to be in bed yourself,' she said quietly. 'You look dreadful.'

If he heard her, he gave no indication of doing so as, wordlessly and without a backward glance, he departed from the kitchen.

A few moments later, armed with the tray, Cassie made her way upstairs. She walked along the landing and nudged open the door on her left with her shoulder.

'Hello.' William raised his head from the pillow and greeted her with a wan smile.

'How do you feel?' Cassie set the tray down on the bedside table. There were two chairs drawn up by the bed, the squashed cushion in one indicating recent occupation. Hmm. Just as she'd suspected. Adam had sat up all night with his nephew. 'Hungry?'

'Not very,' William murmured and, reaching for the tumbler, drank the orange juice. 'Where's Uncle Adam?'

'Having a shower. Try some porridge. Just a bit.'

William shook his head peevishly and burrowed back down beneath the bedclothes. 'I'm still thirsty. And I'm cold.'

'I'll fetch another blanket and some more orange,' Cassie said gently. By the time she returned, William was fast asleep. Careful not to disturb him, she tucked the thick rug she'd discovered in the linen cupboard into the bed and placed the glass of orange juice on the table. Picking up the tray, she moved silently across the room and on to the landing. She started to walk towards the stairs and then paused outside Adam's door. He ought to have showered and changed by now.

She remained motionless, staring at the closed door. She couldn't hear the sound of any movements issuing from inside the room. She grimaced. Adam wouldn't thank her for worrying about him, she reminded herself forcefully. She started to move away and then hesitated. He'd looked so ill... Oh, for Pete's sake, she chided herself swiftly. He obviously had a touch of flu which had doubtless been aggravated by a night's loss of sleep, that's all. He wasn't going to keel over, collapse in the shower.

Swiftly she discarded the tray on the floor and knocked gently on the door. The door hadn't been shut properly and swung open under her touch, revealing the large, sunlit room beyond. Lying on his front, Adam was stretched out on the king-sized bed, his eyes closed.

Cassie swung away, closing the door behind her, her eyebrows knitted together ferociously. Didn't the damn man possess a bath-robe, a pair of pyjamas, a towel?

Did he have to lie stark naked on his bed? Maybe it was
his bedroom and he wasn't expecting visitors but even
so... God... She'd never realised just how beautiful a
man's body could be. She'd only glanced at him for the
merest fraction of a second and yet the image of the
strong, powerful male lines were imprinted with complete and disturbing clarity in her head.

She swallowed, willing her hammering heart to settle
back to normal. Should she just go away, wait for him
to wake up in due course? He was going to end up with
pneumonia, let alone flu, lying there completely un-
covered. Action replay. She thumped loudly on the closed
door and then, hearing no response, opened it a crack.
'Adam?'

She was greeted by continuing silence. Perhaps he was
really ill, had just managed to crawl on to the bed. She
flung open the door and walked briskly across the rich,
chocolate-coloured carpet to the bed. Eyes fixed firmly
on the dark head, she shook his shoulder, instantly conscious of the heat radiating from the smooth skin beneath her palm.

He grunted and then slowly opened his eyes. For a
moment he seemed disorientated, seemed to have trouble
focusing on her face, and then his eyebrows knitted
together in a black line. 'What the hell are you doing in
my bedroom?' he thundered hoarsely. 'Out!'

'Get into bed,' Cassie ordered without preamble.
Gracious to the last, Professor dear. 'You're ill,' she
stated flatly.

Walking across to the window she drew the cream curtains together, blocking out the sunshine. 'And no, I
don't make a habit of creeping into my employers' bed-
rooms. And yes, I know you can't stand bossy females.'

Turning round, she was surprised but gratified to discover that he had obeyed her instructions and was ensconced beneath the cream and brown duvet. 'Would
you like anything?' she enquired. 'A drink?'

There was no answer and, moving closer to the bed, she saw that his eyes were closed again. Sleep softened the harsh contours of his face; he looked gentler, younger, almost vulnerable. She stared down at him, fighting the temptation to smooth back a lock of tousled dark hair that had fallen across the high, proud forehead, and turned away, closing the door quietly behind her.

He hadn't even asked about William, she realised suddenly, her heart flipping over. Not because he'd forgotten his nephew but because he knew that she would take care of William. If he'd doubted her at all, he would never have permitted himself to fall asleep in the first place. Her mouth curved. Despite his constant criticism, his taunting gibes, when it came to the crunch he trusted her.

The knowledge enveloped her like a warm cocoon for the rest of the day, a day that seemed to be spent traipsing endlessly up and downstairs with trays for the two invalids.

William was fractious, demanding, fretting that he wouldn't be recovered in time for the school play. Adam, on the other hand, she mused as she prepared herself for bed that night, had proved to be the model patient. He'd eaten and drunk whatever she'd placed in front of him without demur, thanking her courteously when she returned to collect his tray, although she sensed that he was acting on auto-pilot, going through the motions mechanically.

She slipped on the silk nightdress that she'd bought in Singapore on her stopover back from Australia. She'd sped over to Mead Cottage during the afternoon to collect a few essentials, explain the situation to Kate.

Diving into bed, she turned off the light and gazed up into the darkness. Her eyes began to flicker downwards and then jerked open again. Throwing back the bedclothes, she reached for the switch on her bedside lamp. She'd heard something—William? Demanding yet another drink?

She padded out on to the landing and froze, the hairs rising on the back of her neck as she heard the deep, hoarse cry of despair.

Without thinking, she rushed down the landing and flung open Adam's door. Moonlight filtered through a crack in the curtains, illuminating the figure stirring restlessly in his sleep, threshing against the confines of the bedclothes, mumbling incoherently.

She touched his forehead and her eyes darkened with anxiety. He was burning hot. Darting into the bathroom, she soaked a flannel in cold water and, returning, gently wiped the perspiration from his face. For a moment he lay still and then he began to move again, fighting against her administrations.

'No! For God's sake... Rowena... No!'

Cassie went rigid, the anguish and despair in the cracked voice cutting through her like a knife. What particular nightmare was he reliving in his fevered brain? Rowena's tragic death. Or, even after all these years, had the wound she'd inflicted on him never healed, still had the power to haunt his subconscious?

Her heart constricting, she sat down on the edge of the bed, instinctively cradling his head in her arms, stroking the thick dark hair.

'Shh, it's all right,' she murmured soothingly, and gradually felt him still beneath her touch. Reaching out, she tugged the duvet up over the naked expanse of bronzed chest, as much, she admitted, for her own peace of mind as anything else.

'Thirsty...' he muttered.

She stood up and poured out a glass of water from the jug she'd placed on his table earlier. Cupping her hand behind his neck, she raised the glass to his mouth. He drank thirstily and then his head fell back on the pillow.

She placed the empty glass on the table and jolted as she suddenly felt his hand reach out for hers. 'Don't go.'

His fingers tightened around hers, drawing her back towards the bed,

'My, God, you're so beautiful.'

A pulse started beating erratically at the base of her neck. He was delirious, didn't know what he was saying... As if she were in a trance, she felt his arms reach up, pulling her into the bed beside him.

'I've wanted you from the first time I saw you.' His hand swept possessively down the length of her body as he crushed her against him.

There was no steady rise of warmth, just an explosion of fierce sensuous pleasure as his mouth traced a scalding path down her neck. She could feel every muscle, every sinew of the hard male body through the thin silk of her nightdress. Governed not by rational thought but solely by some dormant primaeval instinct, she arched against him, her hands beginning their own tentative exploration, moving slowly over the hair-roughened chest...

She froze. This was insanity! What the hell was she doing? Adam didn't even know who she was, didn't know who he was holding, caressing. In his confused state she was nothing more than a female body. Any female body. Or was he imagining that it was Rowena lying here beside him?

Recoiling, she struggled from his embrace and leapt out of the bed. He made no effort to stop her and, looking down, she saw his eyes were closed, his chest rising and falling slowly and evenly. How could she have been so stupid as to think for a moment that, even in his feverish state, it was she whom Adam desired? And she had no one else but herself to blame for that tearing ache inside her.

Slowly she walked from the room. All she prayed was that Adam would have no recollection of this in the morning.

CHAPTER EIGHT

PLACING the supper tray on Adam's bedside table, Cassie walked across the room and drew the curtains.

He put down the book she'd fetched from the library that morning, having discovered to her surprise that he shared her liking for thrillers.

'Fish?' Balancing the tray on his knee, he surveyed his meal without enthusiasm. 'Again?'

'Fish is very nutritious,' Cassie snapped. She'd already been through this with William. Casting one disgusted look at the fare on offer, he'd muttered darkly under his breath something about hamburgers and chips and promptly fallen asleep again.

'I thought it was we invalids who were supposed to be fractious, not Nurse,' Adam murmured mildly.

She grinned, looking down at him from the end of the bed. 'I prefer my patients comatose!' With six days' growth of dark stubble covering his jaw, he looked like a marauding pirate.

'What do you think?' Putting down his knife and fork, he ran a lean hand over his chin. 'Shall I keep it? Grow a beard?'

She shrugged, disconcerted that he'd guessed her thought so easily. She liked the square, tenacious jaw. It would be a pity to conceal it, but she very much doubted that he would be influenced by her opinion, despite his idle question. Like William, he had improved greatly over the last two days. His eyes had lost the dull lustre, his face the unnatural pallor.

Her prayer had been answered. He seemed to have absolutely no recollection of that first night, had lain for the following three days in a twilight world of his own. Had no recollection at all of the hours she'd sat by his bed in a silent vigil, listening to his tortured ramblings, cooling his heated skin, aching to cradle him in her arms again.

'Maria phoned again this afternoon while you were asleep to see how you were getting on.' That was the third time in as many days. 'And sends you her love.' Her lips compressed together. She wasn't his social secretary, was getting sick of relaying messages from the faceless, husky-voiced female.

He smiled up at her. 'Maria,' he mused reflectively. 'A brilliant mind.' He swallowed a mouthful of fish. 'English professor,' he added laconically.

'Really?' Cassie murmured with feigned *ennui*. She guessed that a woman would have to be intelligent as well as attractive to appeal to him.

'Married to a physicist.' The blue eyes gleamed. 'Four grown-up sons.'

She picked up the empty tray. She really wasn't the slightest bit interested... He didn't think for one moment that...

'And some woman—I didn't quite catch her name,' she added carelessly, 'Trish? Terri?—brought you round some grapes.'

He folded his arms behind his head. 'Long blonde hair? Slim?'

'Yes,' she said shortly, moving to the door. With about six-foot-long legs, a perfect skin and a row of dazzling white teeth. So he had a penchant for blondes, did he?

'Tina Murray,' he murmured. 'Ben's mum.' He raised a dark eyebrow. 'William's current best friend.'

Why did he keep offering her these explanations? She really wasn't the slightest bit interested in his personal life.

'So where are they?' he drawled as she reached the door.

'Are what?' She frowned.

'The grapes?'

She smiled. 'I've eaten them. We didn't want pips in our bed, now did we?' she added solicitously, and vanished through the door.

Stretching up, Cassie placed the last bauble on the Christmas tree and then stood back to admire her handiwork.

'What do you reckon, Lisa? Pretty artistic, huh?'

The shaggy mongrel stretched out on the hearth by the fire ignored her.

Readjusting a strand of tinsel, Cassie stooped down, plugged the fairy-lights into the wall socket and switched them on. Turning off the main room light and flicking on a table-lamp, she sat cross-legged by the fire, absently stroking Lisa's ears, and surveyed the tree with pleasure. Would William be pleased by his surprise?

He was so much better that she could see no reason why he shouldn't get up for an hour or two tomorrow. She'd bought some crêpe paper as well as the tree, and planned to show him how to make paper streamers, hoping that the activity would compensate in some way for his acute disappointment at missing the school play.

She unfurled her jean-clad legs and stretched them out in front of her. She ought to start thinking about going to bed but, despite her exhausting day, didn't feel tired yet. She sighed contentedly. She couldn't remember when she'd last felt so serene, peaceful. She was enjoying playing nurse, she admitted—although it was a pity her patients had recovered their appetites.

She'd taken William a slice of cherry cake with his bedtime cocoa to compensate for the fish, which, she admitted ruefully, having eaten it herself, had been singularly unappetising. Adam too had seemed equally grateful for the bedtime snack, having first, she recalled with a grin, ascertained that the cake had been purchased from a local bakery and not produced by her.

Her eyes darkened pensively. It was the first time in her life she'd actually been necessary to someone else's well-being, the first time anyone had actually needed her. She pulled a mocking face. That was something of an exaggeration. Adam and William would have managed without her. No doubt Maria or Tina would have rallied round, she thought drily. Still, it was nice to feel ... Oh, admit it ... It was nice to feel, if only temporarily, completely involved in Adam's life, to feel that her presence in his home actually mattered. She brought her knees up to her chest and hugged them.

'Cassandra!'

At the unexpected sound of the deep voice, she whirled round in surprise, could do nothing to stop the swirl of pleasure at the sight of Adam standing in the doorway, clad in his towelling robe, a glass of orange in his hand, even though it had been barely an hour since she'd last seen him. Then, as she absorbed the forbidding expression on his face, her heart plummeted. Her pleasure was evidently not reciprocated. Adam looked anything but pleased to see her, must have assumed that she'd already gone to bed, had expected to find the sitting-room deserted.

'Shouldn't you be getting back to Mead Cottage?' he enquired tersely.

'What?' She looked at him blankly. How could this glowering, remote stranger be the same man who had teased her unmercifully about her culinary skills such a short time ago?

'I had no idea that you were staying this late every night. There is really no need.'

Cassie cleared her throat. 'But I've not been going back ... I'm—er—staying in the spare room.' Surely he must have realised that. Maybe not. Until today he'd been almost completely comatose.

'I see.' His eyes were dark, unreadable, but she could sense his inexplicable and growing hostility. 'I suppose it never occurred to you to ask me first?'

Cassie fought back the hot spurt of anger, deliberately waiting a few seconds before answering. 'No, it didn't,' she said evenly. 'You've been virtually dead to the world since Friday.'

'So you decided to use your initiative, hmm? Move in?' His eyes flickered to the fire. 'You've certainly made yourself at home.' His mouth tightened as his gaze moved to the corner of the room. 'And what's that?'

What the hell did he think it was? 'How about a Christmas tree?' She clicked her fingers together. 'Aw, shucks, I forgot to ask you if I could buy one first.' Turning on her heel she sauntered unhurriedly from the room and then, the minute she was out of sight, ran up the stairs two at a time.

Reaching her room, she threw herself full-length on the bed and pummelled the pillow with her fist in sheer frustration. The temptation to make the grand gesture, pack up her belongings—including the Christmas tree— and storm out of the house was overwhelming.

She'd been completely deluding herself over the past few days, she realised, turning over on her back and staring up at the ceiling. Adam's attitude towards her hadn't changed one whit. He'd simply tolerated her presence because he'd had little choice, had needed someone—anyone—to care for William while he himself was incapacitated.

It was so damn unfair! She'd run around after him as well as William for days now. God knew how many times she'd been up and down those wretched stairs. She didn't want, nor had she expected, Adam's undying gratitude, but to turn on her like that was inexcusable.

She jumped from the bed and paced up and down the room, glaring ferociously down at the carpet. Huh! 'So you decided to use your initiative. Move in.' It made her sound like a squatter. No. It made her sound like a conniving female who had taken advantage of the situation to establish herself in the household. Was that what the contemptible, arrogant worm thought? He should take a long close look at himself. Who in their right mind would live under Adam Merrick's roof through choice, endure his obnoxious presence morning noon and night?

She stiffened, coming to an abrupt halt as she heard the light tap at the bedroom door and the sound of her name. What now? Had he come to evict her forcibly from the premises? She flung the door open. 'Yes?'

Adam raised his hands, palms towards her as if warding off an attack. 'I'm sorry.'

She surveyed him in complete silence for a second and then slammed the door in his face, turning the key noisily in the lock for good measure. Go boil your head, Professor. Did he think one insincere glib 'sorry' made everything all right? He must have suddenly had a twinge of guilt, belatedly realised just how unfair he'd been. But she was blowed if she was going graciously to accept his apology just to salve his conscience. And besides, Adam simply regretted voicing his thoughts out loud. His apology didn't fundamentally change anything, didn't alter the fact that he resented her presence in his home and the fact that he'd been forced to depend on her for a short time.

Despite her conviction to the contrary, she fell into a deep dreamless sleep the moment her head hit the pillow, and awoke early before the alarm went off. Yawning, she climbed out of bed, washed and dressed mechanically, ran a cursory comb through her hair and made her way downstairs. Greeting Lisa with a monosyllabic grunt, she switched on the kettle and tipped dog meal into a bowl while she waited for it to boil. Conscious, coherent thought slowly returned as she took her first sip of tea.

Mug clasped in her hand, she gazed out through the kitchen window up at the dark ominous sky. That was just how she felt today. Grey, gloomy and overcast. So what now? Did she simply carry on with her Florence Nightingale routine as if nothing had happened?

She was beginning to regret slamming the door in Adam's face last night—much though he'd deserved it.

She wished she'd acted with far more maturity and dignity. Instead she'd simply reduced herself to his puerile level.

She would despise herself if she walked out now, she admitted, feel that she'd let William down, deserted him. Decision made, she gulped the remainder of her tea and started on the breakfast preparations.

Some time later, having already attended to William, she tapped on the door of Adam's bedroom, took a deep breath and walked in.

'Good morning.' She discarded the tray and beamed down at him as he opened a brilliant blue eye. 'And how are we today?' she enquired breezily, drawing the curtains.

'Oh, my God!' He gave a loud groan and eased himself into a sitting position. 'It's the lady with the lamp.'

'Now, now,' Cassie tutted disapprovingly. 'We really mustn't go upsetting ourselves like this.'

She smelt a rat. Or at least the distinctive scent of expensive soap. His hair was slightly damp and he was wearing his robe, indicating that he'd only recently emerged from the shower. So he'd been deliberately feigning sleep when she'd first entered the room. Hmm. Was the nice, kind, even-tempered professor becoming accustomed to room service—despite his strong reservations about the waitress?

'Enjoy your breakfast,' she said sweetly. It'll be the last one you have prepared by these fair hands. She began to move towards the door.

'Don't go yet, Cassie. Stay and talk to me while I eat it.'

She stiffened, grateful that her back was towards him as she heard the low, coaxing voice. What was the matter with the man? A few hours ago he couldn't wait to get shot of her. And now...

She turned round slowly, her heart dipping as she met the full force of the brilliant blue eyes, the slow, lazy smile.

'What do you want to talk about? Her voice was casual, slightly bored, betraying nothing of her sudden wariness, uncertainty. She would never be able to fathom out this enigmatic man in a million years. Maybe he wasn't that complex after all. Maybe that aura of strength, assurance, dependability was totally misleading. Perhaps he was completely unstable, subject to erratic, irrational mood swings.

'Tell me what's been happening over the last few days.'

'I've saved all the newspapers. You can read them later,' she answered drily. 'When you get dressed and come downstairs,' she added pointedly.

'You mean we can get up today?' he enquired gravely, looking up from his cereal bowl.

'As we're obviously feeling so much better, yes,' Cassie agreed, couldn't keep her face straight any longer and grinned back at him. Admitting defeat, she pulled up a chair and helped herself to a piece of toast. She was so weak, a traitor to her sex.

'How's Kate? Have she and Richard set a date yet?'

'Beginning of May.' Cassie bit into her toast.

'Presumably Kate will move into Richard's house. So what will you do? Stay on at Mead Cottage on your own?'

Cassie wrinkled her nose. 'I haven't really thought about it yet. May's months away.' She shrugged. 'I don't know what I'll be doing by then . . .'

'Or where you'll be?' Adam murmured quietly.

She looked down at her half-eaten toast, her appetite suddenly vanishing. 'It all depends.' She could sense his eyes on her face, was aware of the sudden inexplicable tension in the room.

'On what, Cassie?'

His voice was so low she barely caught his words. He was playing some sort of game with her, she thought with a rush of panic. It was almost as if he wanted her to admit . . .

She raised her eyes and smiled. 'On whether I get accepted on that cordon bleu cookery course I've applied for.' Find someone else to pander to your over-inflated ego. She rose to her feet and unconsciously crammed the remnants of her toast into the pocket of her jeans.

'Get a bit peckish mid-morning, hmm?'

'Mmm?' Baffled by the undisguised amusement on his face, she picked up the used crockery and headed for the door.

Her forehead creased as she walked down the landing. Fat chance and pigs might fly, but just suppose Adam offered her a permanent job as his secretary—how would she react? Is that what he'd been hinting at? She couldn't believe his arrogance, his implication that he could in any way influence her future plans, as if working for him was all she could ever want from life, the pinnacle of her entire existence. And anyway, surely he wouldn't need a full-time secretary once the university term started again, would he?

'You can put in that last bit,' William murmured magnanimously, handing Cassie a piece of jigsaw.

'Thank you,' she said gravely, conscious of the honour bestowed upon her, and exchanged a quick smile with Adam over the top of the small bowed head.

Adam's eyes dropped to the book on his lap. He was sitting in an armchair by the fire, long legs stretched out across the hearth. She was glad he'd decided not to grow a beard after all, Cassie mused absently, her eyes following the strong contours of his clean-shaven jaw and chin. He looked tired; his first day up had probably drained him of more energy than he would care to admit.

'Go on, then,' William urged impatiently.

'Mmm? Oh, yes.' Cassie slotted in the piece of jigsaw and William gave a sigh of satisfaction.

'Good.' He studied the completed puzzle for a moment and then started to break it up. 'Shall we do another one now?'

'Not tonight, Will.' Adam snapped his book closed and rose to his feet in a swift, controlled movement. 'Time for bed, old chap.'

'But I've been in bed for days and days, Uncle Adam,' William protested automatically but without much conviction in his voice as he dutifully scrambled down from his chair. 'Goodnight, Cassie.' He hugged her and then surveyed her thoughtfully. 'It's nice having you to stay.' He swivelled his head. 'Isn't it, Uncle Adam?'

Cassie concentrated on gathering up the pieces of jigsaw and putting them in the box. There is a great future ahead for you in the diplomatic service, William. Ask me for a reference any time.

'Yes, it is.'

What? Had she heard correctly? Cassie's eyes shot to Adam but his back was turned to her as he shepherded his nephew from the room. Mmm. Adam had been put on the spot then, could hardly do anything but agree with William. Don't start analysing the whole thing, start speculating about a few insignificant words.

She placed the lid on top of the box and moved away from the table. Glancing a little self-consciously back over her shoulder, she stood on tiptoe and peeped in the mirror above the fireplace. A pair of large luminous grey eyes regarded her pensively. Lord, her hair was a mess. Come to think of it, she hadn't touched it since first thing this morning. She ran a hand through the red curls but they refused to be subdued and sprang back in a wilful halo around her small, flushed face.

Shrugging, she made her way into the kitchen, switched on the kettle and set out two mugs. She stretched her hands above her head and yawned. Today must be a record. Except for one brief excursion into town for groceries, she'd spent practically the entire day in Adam's company and he hadn't bitten her head off once.

They'd spent a couple of hours this morning in his office, ostensibly catching up on his correspondence, but in actuality had spent most of the time talking. She wrinkled her nose. At least, she, not normally prone to garrulousness, had talked. Prompted by Adam's questions, she had virtually related her entire life history. For some inexplicable reason, she remembered with a jolt of unease, she'd even told him about that day, all those years ago, when she'd stood listening to her relatives discussing her future. That was something she had never told another living soul. Not even Kate.

William had come downstairs after lunch and had been gratifyingly enchanted with the Christmas tree and enthusiastic about her suggestion that they make paper streamers, an enthusiasm which, to her secret delight, Adam had seemed to share.

The three of them had sprawled on the carpet surrounded by crêpe paper, making teasing, disparaging remarks about each other's creative efforts... They had seemed to spend the entire afternoon laughing, although she couldn't now remember for the life of her at what.

Heaving a sigh of pure contentment, Cassie carried the mugs through to the sitting-room.

Adam was sitting on the settee, dark head thrown back, absorbed in thought. Cassie's eyes wandered over his face. She loved the way his eyes darkened almost to navy blue when he was thinking, concentrating, the way they lit up with laughter when he was amused. The corners of her mouth tugged into a wry smile. Not so keen on the way they turned the colour of granite when he was angry. She would never tire of looking at him, she thought with a painful dip of her stomach.

'Thanks.' He gave her a lazy smile as she handed him his mug. Hesitating only briefly she sat down beside him.

'Like a brandy with it?' he enquired.

'Better not if I'm driving.' She was deliberately fishing and she knew it. There was no necessity for her to spend another night here. Adam and William, if not a hundred per cent fit, were certainly capable of fending for them-

selves now. Although of course if he asked her to stay...
She held her breath.

'You're probably right,' he murmured easily, and she
swallowed back the spurt of disappointment. Rising to
his feet, he crossed the room to the unobtrusive drinks
cabinet, helped himself to a small measure of brandy
and rejoined her on the sofa. He took a sip. 'I was pretty
much out for the count the first few days, wasn't I?' he
suddenly demanded abruptly, turning towards her, his
gaze intent.

'Yes.'

He was silent for a moment but his eyes never strayed
from her face. 'Did I ramble much?'

Cassie met the level, measured gaze squarely. 'Yes.'
She knew how much he would hate that knowledge, but
knew too that she couldn't lie to him. 'You talked about
Rowena,' she said quietly.

'I see.' Betraying no emotion at all, he tossed the re-
mains of the brandy down his throat.

Cassie took a deep breath. 'Adam,' she said tentatively, 'what happened?' She flinched as she saw his eyebrows draw together, the muscles clenching in the strong
jaw, steeling herself for the harsh rebuff. Then as she
witnessed the shooting, stabbing pain in his eyes, she
cursed herself, awash with shame that she had forced
him yet again to relive the agony of the past simply to
satisfy her own curiosity.

'I'm sorry... I shouldn't have...'

'No.' His voice was so low she barely heard it. 'I'd
like to tell you.' There was a long silence and then he
leant back against the sofa, his eyes focused directly
ahead. 'I was lecturing at a university in the north of
England. My first post.' He paused. 'One of my students failed her end of term exams.' His voice grew
brittle. 'She came to me and offered me certain favours
in return for upgrading her paper.' Abruptly he rose to
his feet and poured another brandy. 'I declined the offer.'

Cassie's eyes flew to his face. So that was why he had been so inordinately touchy about Susan...

'A few days later, Rowena received an anonymous letter informing her that I was having an affair with one of my students.' His mouth tightened. 'I was too proud, too stubborn even to deny her accusations. I thought if she didn't trust me, believed that I would be such a damn fool as to get involved with a student, what the hell was the point?'

His fingers gripped the stem of the brandy glass, his knuckles whitening. 'No.' His voice had dropped an octave, was so low that Cassie had to strain her ears to hear it. 'It was nothing to do with hurt pride. I'd known for some time that I didn't want to spend the rest of my life with Rowena, that I'd confused physical attraction with love.' His mouth curled in self-contempt. 'I used the whole sordid situation to my advantage. When she broke off the engagement I felt nothing but relief.'

He rose to his feet and began to pace jerkily around the room. 'The next thing I knew she wrote to me announcing she was going to marry Andrew. The marriage didn't stand a snowball's chance in hell. I knew damn well she'd only married Andrew as some sort of revenge and he was on the rebound from Kate.'

Kate had broken off the relationship with Andrew! Cassie absorbed the information incredulously. All that wasted guilt...

'Last Christmas we all gathered at my parents' home as usual.' He came to an abrupt halt in front of the fireplace. 'Rowena decided to pay me a courtesy call at two o'clock in the morning. Not to put too fine a point on it, I told her to go to hell.' His mouth twisted. 'Hardly the subtlest of rejections but it wasn't the first time...' He slumped back down on the sofa. 'A few days later Andrew turned up on my doorstep and accused me of having an affair with Rowena for the past six years.' The bitterness in the harsh voice made Cassie shudder. 'She had apparently informed him I was William's father.'

'Oh, my God.'

'Rowena appeared some time later. She tried to pacify Andrew, admitted she'd been taunting him deliberately, but the damage had been done. He stormed out of the house, Rowena behind him.' His face was ashen. 'Andrew drove into a tree and they were both killed instantaneously.'

'I'm so, so sorry.' Cassie's voice shook with compassion.

He hadn't even heard her, was still in his own tormented world. 'I should have stopped him . . . taken his car keys . . . I knew he was in no fit state to drive . . . but at the time I was so angry . . .'

The raw naked emotion on his face was more than she could bear. 'It wasn't your fault . . .' Without thinking, desperate only to ease his pain, she reached out for his hand.

'Wasn't it?' he said hoarsely.

'No!' she said fiercely. 'If anybody . . .'

'Rowena?' he said harshly. 'My God, the times I've hated her as much as myself . . .' For a second he remained as still and expressionless as a statue hewn out of rock and then, his hand tightening around hers, he pulled Cassie on to his lap, pressing her so tightly against his chest that she thought she was going to suffocate.

As his hold on her lessened, she looked up at him, her eyes wide and vulnerable, drowning in the deep blue depths. And in that imperceptible moment the atmosphere changed, became charged with electricity.

Lowering his head, he brushed her forehead with his lips, moved slowly over her cheekbones. Eyes closed, Cassie's arms reached up and curled around his neck, warm, drugging pleasure seducing her raw nerve-endings as his mouth outlined the whirl of her ear, traced a scalding path down her arched neck.

Lost in a whirlpool of sensation, she swayed against him, a feeling of overwhelming relief shuddering through her as his mouth finally took possession of hers.

His hand moved caressingly down the length of her body and then slid beneath her sweatshirt, his fingers moving in lingering, sensuous circles over her ribcage. Then with tantalising slowness his hand moved upwards, closed over the swelling cups of her breasts, his thumb brushing teasingly over the hardening nipples.

Cassie stirred against him, the longing to feel his hand against her bare heated skin almost unbearable. His kiss deepened, became more insistent, his tongue exploring the inner moistness between her soft, parted lips.

'Oh, God... I want... I need to make love to you.' His voice was hoarse as he picked her up in his arms and laid her gently full-length on the carpet.

Head spinning, she offered no resistance as he eased her sweatshirt over her head and unfastened the single clasp of her bra, gasping with delighted shock as she felt the warmth of his mouth on her breast, his tongue flicking over the throbbing rosy peak.

Her hands fumbled at the buttons of his shirt, pushing it aside, shivering as the tips of her breasts brushed against the hard wall of his chest. His mouth moved downwards, over the soft silkiness of her stomach to the waistband of her jeans. She heard the sound of a zip as he pulled the jeans over her slender hips, sighing as his fingers slid beneath the lace briefs, stroking her, caressing her until they reached the pulsating heated moistness of her innermost being.

'Adam,' she mumbled, need exploding through her, her eyes beseeching him to remove the remaining hindrance between them. She heard the rustle of clothes and her gaze moved down the deep chest, followed the trail of fine dark hair, her mouth going dry as she witnessed the physical evidence of his own urgent desire.

Hesitantly, and then with growing confidence, her hands moved over the taut hard male body, heard his muffled groan as her mouth closed over the warm skin.

His knee moved between her legs, nudging them apart, his breathing shallow and erratic as he lowered his weight between the hot dampness of her thighs. Instinctively her body began to move against his...

'Cassie——' his voice was hoarse, urgent in her ear '—I'm not prepared. Are you on the Pill...?'

'No,' she whispered, 'but...'

With a low, anguished moan, Adam moved off her. 'I won't be responsible for fathering an unwanted child.' His breathing was harsh, ragged.

'It doesn't matter...' Adam's child, Cassie thought dazedly, reaching out to him, aching for that final fulfilment. The most precious thing in the world. 'It wouldn't be...'

She stiffened, her eyes opening as she felt him push her hand away roughly. Uncomprehendingly she looked at him as he reached for his jeans and rose abruptly to his feet. What had happened? What had she done wrong? she wondered desperately as she saw the cold, forbidding expression on his face.

'How crass of me not to have realised.' As his eyes moved over her, she grabbed for a sweatshirt. Anything to cover her, to shield her from those contemptuous blue eyes.

'Of course "it wouldn't be"!' he rasped. 'There wouldn't be a child at all, would there? I was forgetting the alternatives...'

What? The meaning of his words finally sank into her confused, muddled brain. He meant abortion. 'No!' Eyes wide with stunned horror, her hand moved protectively across her abdomen, as if warding off an attack.

'Oh, come on, Cassie,' he sneered. 'Just think how pregnancy, let alone a child, would impinge on your lifestyle.'

She couldn't believe that this was happening. Couldn't believe that they were fighting about a hypothetical situation that would now never arise; that this remote stranger with the taunting blue eyes was the man who had a few seconds ago reduced her to fever pitch with his coaxing, expert hands and mouth. He now looked as if he hated her.

'Get dressed,' he said curtly, striding towards the door. 'I'll order a taxi. It should be here by the time you've packed up your belongings.' He paused. 'Oh, and tell Kate that I'll contact her in the New Year if I require another secretary.'

Numb with shock, Cassie stared at the closed door. So that was that. Out of Adam's home. Out of his life. She almost cried out aloud as the first wave of tearing pain washed over her.

CHAPTER NINE

FIVE whole days. It was Christmas Eve and she had wasted five whole days. Hands sunk into the pockets of her jacket, collar drawn up against the wind, Cassie walked along the river tow-path. It had been obvious enough after the first day that Adam had no intention of contacting her but still she'd gone on hoping, jumping every time the telephone rang or the doorbell pealed. Talk about the eternal optimist! Or the biggest fool in the world.

She stooped down, picked up a pebble and tossed it into the river, watching the ripples grow wider and wider. She'd made herself a virtual prisoner at Mead Cottage. Until this morning, except for a brief excursion to buy Christmas presents, she'd hardly put her nose out of the door. It was bad enough losing sleep over a man, but to lose her days as well!

She increased her pace, swinging her arms by her sides to keep warm, her stride faltering as she rounded the river bend. A tall dark-haired man, a small muffled figure by his side, was throwing bread to the ducks.

This was her place. He had no right to be here... The man turned his head as he murmured something to the child, and she saw the dark moustache and glasses. Relief and disappointment warred for supremacy as Cassie turned round abruptly and started to retrace her steps.

It was time she was getting back anyway. Kate was going to Richard's office party at lunchtime, Mary had been given the afternoon off, so Cassie had promised to hold the fort. Not that Kate had envisaged many callers so near to the start of the festive holiday.

Arriving back at Mead Cottage, she changed out of her jeans and sweatshirt into a pink sweater and an old

navy skirt she'd found at the back of her wardrobe. She
sat down on the edge of the bed to slip on her court
shoes, and her eyes fell on the pile of wrapped parcels
piled up in a chair. What was she going to do with
William's present?

Her eyes darkened uneasily. Why hadn't she simply
asked Richard to drop off the parcel at Adam's cottage
next time he was passing?

The most natural course of action would have been
to take over the present herself, but she'd shied away
from that, dreading that Adam might misinterpret her
motive in doing so. She bit her lip. And would he be
right? Had she subconsciously been hanging on to
William's gift because it provided her with an excuse to
go over to the cottage...and see Adam? She was no
better than Susan, the student who had used her assignment as an excuse to gain access to him, she thought
with revulsion.

She knocked on Kate's office door and walked in.
'Thought I'd come down a bit early. Give you more time
to change,' she murmured as her aunt looked up from
her desk.

'Thanks, Cass.' Kate closed the file on her desk and
stood up. 'Hope you won't get too bored. It's bound to
be very quiet this afternoon.'

'I've come prepared,' Cassie smiled, indicating the
writing paper and envelopes in her hand.

She walked out into the reception area, settled down
at Mary's desk and picked up her pen. She wrote to four
universities requesting their prospectuses for the next
academic year, and then dashed off a note to the overseas
employment agency in London, advising them that she
was looking for temporary casual employment anywhere in Europe from the beginning of January.

Sitting back in her chair, she surveyed the five sealed
envelopes with satisfaction. At last she had done something positive about her future, although she didn't
expect an immediate response to her final letter. At this

time of year, most seasonal employment would be centred in the skiing resorts and she'd left it far too late to apply for any vacancies there.

'Good afternoon. Cassandra.'

The hairs on the nape of her neck rose, an icy finger trailing down her spine. The last voice in the world she'd expected or wanted to hear. He must have opened the outer door noiselessly, moved silently across the carpet, giving her absolutely no warning at all of his entry.

Schooling her face into a mask of complete indifference, she slowly raised her eyes. 'Hello, Adam.' What malicious quirk of fate had brought him into the office this afternoon of all afternoons? 'Did you want to see Kate? I'm afraid she's not in the office this afternoon.' She was amazed at her self-control. Her voice held just the right note of courteous, brisk impersonality. 'Can I help at all?'

'I received a copy of my account this morning.' Reaching into a pocket in his jacket, he tossed a sheet of paper on to the desk. 'It's incorrect.'

Cassie felt her hackles beginning to rise at the cold, peremptory tone in his voice, welcomed the wave of indignant anger that surged through her because it momentarily blocked out every other emotion. Was he implying that the agency had over-charged him, that she herself had deliberately miscalculated the number of hours she'd worked for him?

She spread out the sheet of headed paper in front of her and then hid her shaking hands under the desk. 'It seems to be perfectly in order,' she said coolly, perusing the detailed, carefully itemised bill.

'Look at the date the account was closed,' he ordered her tersely and, swinging away from the desk, moved across the carpet to the window, standing with his back to her. 'I haven't been billed for the last seven days.'

Cassie's eyes leapt to the broad shoulders. He hadn't seriously expected to be charged for the time she'd spent at the cottage last week, had he? She'd looked after him

and William while they had flu because she cared about
them, hadn't wanted or expected financial reward. Her
time had been given freely and willingly out of
friendship...

Her throat constricted. No. Not out of friendship. Out
of love. Her dazed eyes moved lingeringly over the tall
figure. I think I've loved you since the moment I saw
you...except that can't be true because I don't believe
in love at first sight. Summoning every ounce of control,
she fought back the swirl of wild hysteria, fought to
regain her composure. She swallowed hard. 'I wasn't actually employed by the agency that week,' she finally
murmured evasively.

Adam swung back round to face her. 'Oh, I see.'

Eyes dark with incomprehension, Cassie dropped her
gaze to her hands, wound together tightly in her lap.
What exactly had he meant by that? Somehow he'd
managed to give the three simple words a wealth of
hidden meaning, make them sound so derogatory.

She watched him from under her lashes as he sat down
in one of the chairs that lined the opposite wall and pulled
out a cheque-book and pen from his pocket. He was so
tantalisingly close and yet so completely out of her reach.
Hungrily her eyes wandered over the strong contours of
his face, committing every feature to memory as if it
might be the last time she would ever see him

'Thank you.' She forced the words out as he rose to
his feet and handed her a cheque. 'I'll write you out a
receipt,' she began, and then faltered as she saw the
second cheque. It was made out not to the agency but
directly to her.

Her eyes shot to his face. 'But——'

'That should cover your time. Naturally I've de-
ducted a certain amount for board and lodging, but I
think you'll agree I've been more than fair.'

For a moment, Cassie felt as if she'd completely
stopped functioning. Not for thirteen years had she felt
this intensity of tearing, raw, agonising pain. She was

nine years old again, numb with hurt and shock. Her hand clenched under the table. She didn't care about Adam. She didn't care about anyone except Kate.

Her hand shaking, she scribbled out a receipt and handed it over to Adam, watching with blank, shuttered eyes as he turned on his heel and crossed the carpet to the outer door.

The moment she heard the door slam shut, she picked up her personal cheque and tore it to shreds.

She succumbed to flu the day after Boxing Day, a mild dose that left her virtually recovered after two days in bed, but provided her with the excuse she needed to escape Richard's New Year's Eve party. A party to which, she'd gleaned from Kate, Adam had, inevitably, also been invited.

She simply did not want to see him, hear his voice again for as long as she lived. He was an intelligent, perceptive man. He knew he'd hurt her and had done so deliberately and callously. And without cause.

He obviously regretted that their relationship had strayed even marginally from the purely platonic, didn't want to pursue it any further, but surely he could have given her credit for working that one out for herself? There had been no need for him to spell it out to her with such insensitive cruelty. But then Adam was an expert in the short, sharp shock treatment, wasn't he? she thought disdainfully, remembering the charade he'd enacted in front of Susan.

Smelling of fragrant soap, clad in the silky emerald dressing-gown Kate had given her for Christmas, Cassie curled up on the sofa, stroking the somnolent cat on her lap. Adam would have probably arrived at Richard's party by now. Alone? She gritted her teeth. She didn't want to think about him dancing with some faceless woman, holding her in his arms, kissing her as Big Ben chimed the hour. Pain twisted through her like a knife as, despite her resolve, the images formed in her head.

She cursed as she heard the doorbell. Who on earth could it be at this time of night? She'd ignore it. Probably some New Year's Eve reveller who had come to the wrong address and would go away when they realised their mistake.

The bell pealed again, louder, more insistently. It could, she supposed, just conceivably be Kate returning to collect something and without a key. Unlikely but ...

Unfurling her bare legs, she sighed and padded onto the landing and down the stairs to the back door. Slipping on the chain, she cautiously opened the door a fraction. Oh, God. Not you. Her eyes widened in pure dismay as they looked up at the tall shadowy figure.

'What do you want?' she demanded brusquely. Go away. Just go away. I don't want to see you.

'May I come in, Cassie? I'd like to talk to you.'

Cassie shook her head. She wasn't going to listen to that deep, persuasive voice. 'I'm very busy. Washing my hair,' she added sarcastically.

'Please, Cassie.'

She hesitated and then slipped off the chain and turned away. 'Shut the door behind you,' she snapped over her shoulder as she retreated up the stairs, tightening the sash of her robe more securely around her waist.

Reaching the sitting-room, she sank down on the sofa and surveyed Adam coolly. 'Well? she demanded.

'May I sit down?' he enquired drily.

She shrugged nonchalantly.

Raising a dark eyebrow, he removed his jacket, revealing a blue silk shirt beneath, and sat down in the armchair opposite her, crossing one dark, expertly tailored leg over the other.

'I've just come from Richard's. Kate told me you'd had flu.' He paused. 'I was concerned.'

'Really?' she said witheringly. 'Concerned for an ex-employee. I'm touched.' Her eyes snapped. 'Why did you really come here tonight, Adam?'

'Because I damn well wanted to see you.' With an incoherent oath, Adam jumped to his feet and started to pace around the room with uncharacteristically jerky strides. 'William's missed you,' he growled, swinging around to face her, eyebrows drawn in a thunderous line across his face. 'And so have I.'

Her eyes dilated with panic as he dropped to the sofa beside her and picked up her hand. She tried to draw away but the blue eyes were beginning to mesmerise her, trapping her like a rabbit in the full glare of headlights. She shivered as she felt the strong, lean fingers stroke the back of her hand in small, sensuous circles, sliding up inside the sleeve of her robe, caressing the delicate skin of her forearm. 'The cottage hasn't been the same since you left,' he muttered huskily. 'I suppose I'd become used to having you around.'

'You've missed me? Got used to having me around?' Cassie snatched her hand away, cursing her moment of temporary weakness as she leapt to her feet. 'What do you think I am? A pet cat? A dog?' She could hear her voice rising but didn't care. 'You march in here and expect ... Go to hell!' She flung open the door, holding it wide. 'Get out.' Of my home and my life. 'Just get out!'

Unhurriedly he rose to his feet and then paused in the doorway.

'Happy New Year, Cassie,' he drawled, his face a blank mask as he towered over her.

She stared up at him in rigid disbelief. He sounded as controlled, as unruffled as if he were taking his leave after a pleasant dinner party.

'I'll call you tomorrow,' he murmured easily.

'What?' she whipped round but he had already gone.

Adam telephoned her three times in as many days to invite her out to dinner and each time she refused point-blank. The thought of sharing a candle-lit meal with him in intimate surroundings was one she wasn't going to entertain even for a second.

What the hell was he playing at? Was it simply that, since her display of complete indifference on New Year's Eve, he now regarded her as a challenge? Her mouth tightened. But she wasn't going to capitulate, wasn't going to lay herself open to being hurt yet again.

And when was he finally going to acknowledge defeat? she wondered as she picked up the telephone on the fourth day and heard the deep, assured voice in her ear.

'Cassie? It's the last day of William's school holidays today,' he began with preamble. 'And I've managed to get tickets for the pantomime in Southampton this afternoon. *Peter Pan*.' There was a slight pause. 'Three tickets.'

Cassie's mouth curved involuntarily. It was years since she'd been to the pantomime and *Peter Pan* was most definitely her favourite. 'No, thank you, Adam,' she said curtly.

'William is going to be very disappointed. I told him I was going to ask you.'

Cassie drew a quick breath. 'You bastard! That's——'

'Blackmail?' Adam enquired cheerfully. 'I know. Despicable, hmm? Right. I'll pick you up at one o'clock.' Before she had time to respond, the line went dead.

Slowly Cassie replaced the receiver on the hook. What harm would it really do to go to the pantomime? She longed to see William again anyway. Her eyes darkened, her heart hammering in her ribcage. Nearly as much as she ached to see Adam, she admitted drearily.

Adam was prompt. As she heard the doorbell peal, Cassie smoothed the green dress over her hips, grabbed her jacket and handbag, and made her way downstairs.

Adam made no comment on her appearance as she opened the door but, as she witnessed the undisguised male appreciation in his eyes, she was irritated to find herself blushing slightly. She hadn't worn the dress for him; it had been her only real alternative to her old navy skirt or jeans.

William was less restrained than his uncle. 'You've got a dress on,' he exclaimed in disbelief after greeting her rapturously. 'Never mind,' he added inexplicably. He caught hold of her hand, tugging her towards the red estate car. 'Sit in the back with me.'

'There's more leg room in the front,' Adam murmured with an innocent grin as he opened the car door for her.

'Cassie doesn't need much room for her legs,' William said witheringly.

She hid her grin and ruffled the small dark head. 'You silver-tongued smoothie.'

'Toss for it, Will.' Carelessly Adam produced a coin from his pocket and spun it deftly into the air as William called his option. 'Heads, old chap. Sorry.' He looked down into Cassie's bemused face. 'I win.'

As Cassie met the dark blue eyes, a tiny shiver crawled down her spine. He was merely being flippant, amusing William. She was being ridiculous to read any underlying significance into his casual declaration of victory, had imagined that note of challenge in his voice. Slipping into the front passenger seat, she fastened her seatbelt with unsteady hands.

She began to relax as the car moved smoothly out into the road. It was impossible not to be affected by William's mounting excitement, and his non-stop chatter spared her from having to make any attempt at superficial conversation with Adam.

He was a skilful driver, she admitted, as they approached the outskirts of Southampton, her eyes dropping to the strong, lean fingers resting lightly around the steering-wheel. And a considerate one, she added mentally. He'd chosen a car renowned primarily for its safety features rather than for high performance and outward ostentatiousness. That choice reflected the man, she mused idly. Adam had nothing to prove to anyone.

He managed to find a space in the car park situated nearest to the theatre, and they were comfortably ensconced in their seats in plenty of time for the start of the performance.

As the lights dimmed, the curtain rose and J.M. Barrie's tale of the boy who never grew up began to unfold on the stage, Cassie quickly became lost in a world of remembered enchantment.

From time to time she glanced at William, her enjoyment intensified as she saw the absorbed expression of his face, an expression, she saw with gentle amusement, that was reflected on his uncle's face.

William was enthralled by the flying sequences, hissed with alarming ferocity when Captain Hook appeared on stage, and let out a small gasp of horror when Tinkerbell drank the poison intended for Peter. When the principal boy wistfully asked the audience if they believed in fairies, he clapped his small hands together with all his might, as if the burden of saving Tinkerbell's life rested on him alone. And Cassie, sitting by his side, threw herself into the performance with equal, unselfconscious enthusiasm.

'I think you enjoyed that more than William did,' Adam murmured to her with a teasing smile as he shepherded his unnaturally subdued nephew through the theatre doors into the chill evening air.

'Certainly as much,' Cassie agreed, fastening the buttons of her coat and pulling on her gloves as they began to walk back towards the car park. And you did your fair share of hissing and clapping, Professor Merrick!

'Hungry?' Adam enquired as he unlocked the car door. 'Why don't you come back and have supper with us? Mrs Evans has left a casserole in the oven.'

Cassie hesitated and then, persuaded by William's enthusiastic endorsement of his uncle's casual invitation, acquiesced. 'Thank you. I'd love to.' It would be churlish to refuse and besides, she admitted, she would feel inordinately flat if Adam simply deposited her at Mead Cottage on the return journey, leaving a long, empty evening looming before her.

'I think that Mrs Evans might just conceivably have the edge over me in the cooking stakes,' Cassie murmured sadly as she placed her knife and fork together on her empty plate. The casserole had been superb.

'Never mind,' William said consolingly. He was sitting opposite her at the kitchen table, already bathed and clad in his pyjamas and dressing-gown. 'You're much prettier than she is.'

'Thank you, kind sir.' Cassie inclined her head graciously in his direction. That glass of wine seemed to have gone straight to her head.

'Come on, Will. Time for bed. School tomorrow.' Adam rose to his feet.

William emitted the obligatory groan, kissed Cassie goodnight and trailed out of the kitchen after his uncle.

Pity to waste the last drop of wine in the bottle, Cassie mused idly, and poured it into her glass. She took an appreciative sip and leant back in her chair. She felt almost too comfortable to move, enveloped in a rosy glow of utter well-being, completely at peace with herself and the world. Draining her glass, she rose reluctantly to her feet and rather absently began to collect up the dirty crockery and place it in the sink.

By the time Adam returned she had washed up and was drying the cutlery.

'Hey, you don't need to do that. Mrs Evans will see to it in the morning,' he murmured.

'Force of habit, I suppose.' She smiled up at him as he gently extracted the tea-towel from her hand, conscious of just how close he was.

'Habits,' he mused, looking down at her upturned face. 'Easy to acquire and hellish to break.' He touched her cheek. 'I think, Miss Cassandra Richardson, that you could very easily become a habit with me.'

'Could I?' She shouldn't have drunk the wine, shouldn't be gazing at him with wide, deliberately provocative eyes.

'I'm afraid so. A rather addictive one.'

Her mouth curved. Mmm. She rather liked the sound of that. Nearly as much as she liked the feel of his mouth brushing against hers. As he drew her unresistingly into his arms, her hands curved up around his neck and she murmured a low sigh of contentment. She shouldn't be letting this happen again, she thought dreamily, but who cared? All that really mattered was Adam and here and now.

Her eyes closed, the contentment changing swiftly to deep, driving need as the pressure of his mouth intensified.

'Cassie.' Adam lifted his head. 'I think coffee might be a good idea,' he said unsteadily, gently releasing his hold.

She nodded, her pupils dilated, a pulse beating erratically at the base of her neck. 'I'll p-put the kettle——'

Her words drowned in her throat as with a muffled groan he pulled her into his arms again. 'I've been aching to do this all day.' As he moulded her into the length of his hard frame, she felt a shudder run through him, heard him expel a long, ragged breath. 'I wanted you from the moment I saw you.'

'What?' Cassie jerked her head up, searching his face, her surprise changing to incredulity as she saw the expression in the dark blue eyes.

'Do you know what it was like...? Working with you day after day...when all I wanted was to touch you...hold you...' he muttered hoarsely, covering her face with tiny, heated kisses.

'You certainly had the oddest way of showing it,' Cassie mumbled through a wave of delirious happiness. Don't please let this be a dream, a wine-induced fantasy.

Moving over to a chair, he pulled her on to his lap. 'I was angry. With you. With myself. The number of times I regretted ever contacting Kate's agency.' He tucked a stray red curl behind her ear. 'You were a complication in my life I didn't need or want.'

'A complication?' she enquired with mock indignation, caressing his face with a gentle, loving hand.

He nodded. 'Above all else, and much as I wanted you, I had to think of William. He's very fond of you, is growing more and more attached to you all the time.'

Cassie frowned. Surely the fact that she and William had a good rapport made things easier, not more complicated?

'If it hadn't been for him, I would never have let you leave the cottage. I'd have persuaded you to stay somehow. Asked you to move in with me.'

'Move in with you?' Cassie repeated slowly. Her euphoria was slipping away, unease like an ominous dark cloud hovering over her.

'As in come and live with me,' Adam said softly. 'No ties. No long-term commitment. Just for however long the arrangement suited us both.'

As his hold on her tightened, Cassie stiffened, pinpricks of fear and dread tingling down her spine. No ties. No commitment. He was joking, teasing her... couldn't possibly be serious...

'But that wouldn't be fair on William. A child needs stability, permanency.'

Cassie wondered if she'd stopped breathing completely. She couldn't seem to move, think straight. She felt sick, deathly cold.

'I—um—think I'll make that coffee now.' She forced the words out through her stiff lips, and slipped off his lap.

In a trance, she moved across the kitchen and filled up the kettle at the sink. Adam hadn't spoken one word of love, given no indication that he even cared about her. He desired her, that was all. Wanted her simply to satiate a temporary physical need.

She clenched her teeth together, fighting back the wave of nausea. Did he think that if he had seriously invited her to live with him, she would have for one moment even considered the sort of relationship he was suggesting, let alone accepted it? Moved into his home and his bed until he grew tired of her? Was that why he had never married? Until the advent of William into his life, had he simply had a succession of casual live-in lovers?

He hadn't invited her to live with him because it wouldn't be fair on William! What about fair on her? she wanted to scream at him. The sheer irony of the situation struck her with sudden force. It was she who had spent her entire adult life avoiding long-term commitments, living from day to day, recoiling from the very thought of being tied down to any one place or person indefinitely. And now her whole philosophy had backfired on her with a vengeance.

The only consolation in this whole awful mess was that at least her pride was relatively intact. She hadn't done or said anything to indicate that her feelings for Adam ran any deeper than his own shallow ones for her.

Summoning every ounce of will power in her being, she turned around and faced him. 'I had a letter from my employment agency in London this morning,' she said casually. 'There's been an unexpected staff vacancy in an hotel in Saas Fee.' Coincidentally she'd worked in the Swiss alpine resort two summers ago. She shrugged. 'It's a family-run business and one of the daughters has been rushed to hospital with appendicitis, so they urgently need an extra pair of hands. It's the busiest time of the year and...' She stopped, aware that she was beginning to ramble.

'I see.' The blue shutters slammed down over his eyes. 'Are you going to go?' His voice was devoid of all emotion.

'Yes.' She'd hadn't been a hundred per cent sure until now.

'And when do you leave?'

He really doesn't care a damn, she thought numbly, wasn't going to make even the slightest attempt to dissaude her. 'As soon as I can arrange a flight.' Tonight, this minute if I could. She swallowed. 'I think I'll skip the coffee, Adam.'

'As you wish.' He rose to his feet abruptly. 'I'll order a taxi.'

She watched him leave the kitchen, wondering how it was possible to love and hate someone with such intensity at the same time.

CHAPTER TEN

CASSIE tugged a thick sweater over her head and walked across the bedroom to the glass door leading out on to the tiny balcony. Turning the key, she stepped outside. The cold, crisp early morning air stung her cheeks and she hugged her arms around her slight body for warmth. Her attic room in the hotel was small, basically furnished, and it was inconvenient having to traipse down to the floor below with her washbag to use the staff bathroom. But the view from the balcony was compensation enough.

Snow-covered pastures extended for about a quarter of a mile beyond the southern edge of the village and rose dramatically into a gigantic wall of glaciers and mountains that formed part of the Mischabel chain. As Cassie's eyes moved slowly over the towering peaks that included the Dom, the highest mountain entirely within the Swiss border, she recited their names in her head, paying homage to their awe-inspiring magnificence.

She started to shiver. A harsh, bleak, alien white world. Saas Fee in the winter was a completely different place to the one in which she'd spent the summer months two years ago. Then the meadows had been covered in a profusion of wild flowers instead of snow. It had been possible to hike for miles along the well-marked mountain trails instead of being restricted to the paths in the vicinity of the village. She missed seeing the grazing cows, missed not being able to climb up to Spielboden on her afternoons off to spend a couple of lazy hours sitting on a rock in the sun, watching the antics of the tame colony of marmots that lived near the lift stop.

She dived back into the warmth of her room, locking the door behind her. She was, she reflected, beginning to get a little sick of snow. Doubtless if she were a ski addict she would view it differently, but the sport had never appealed to her. She smoothed down the duvet on her single bed and hung her towel near the radiator to dry. And, she added wryly, she was becoming more than a little bored with her duties, the endless round of making beds and cleaning rooms that left her physically exhausted at the end of the day but with no real sense of achievement or fulfilment.

She was lonely too, she admitted. The hotelier and his family were warm-hearted and friendly but their English was limited and, although her German had improved during the last eight weeks, it precluded anything but the most elementary of conversations. And because her duties were domestic and didn't include waitressing or serving in the bar, she had little contact with the hotel guests.

She sat down on the edge of her bed and extracted the letter she'd received from Kate that morning from the pocket of her jeans. As she read it through again, a wave of homesickness surged through her. She wished with all her heart she were back at Mead Cottage right now, sitting in the kitchen chatting to Kate. Cupping her chin in her hands, she stared unseeingly at the blank wall in front of her. Was her rootless, aimless, nomadic lifestyle finally beginning to pall?

Her mouth curved in a slow, mocking smile. Talk about a self-pitying grouch. And on her day off! She sighed mournfully. That was the basic cause of this bout of depression. She didn't particularly want a day off. It gave her too many hours in which to have to pretend to be enjoying herself, too many hours of solitude in which to think. And inevitably her thoughts would turn to Adam.

Running away from him hadn't achieved anything. The pain inside her hadn't eased. In fact it seemed to have intensified. But then, what did she really expect? A miracle cure in just over two months? Abruptly she scrambled to her feet.

Right. So how was she going to spend the day? She could walk down to Saas Grund, the small town situated in the valley below Saas Fee, via the Kapellenweg, or Path of the Chapels, she supposed. It was a path she had taken several times already, but the string of fifteen tiny chapels along the route, each containing a group of carved and painted wooden figures, held a continuing fascination. Or maybe she would go further afield, catch a PTT bus from the depot at the end of the Saas Fee— automobile traffic was banned from entering the village itself—and go to Brig, a much larger town and one which she had yet to explore.

Considering her options, Cassie pulled on a second pair of socks, slipped her feet into her snowboots and collected her warm, multi-coloured anorak from the wardrobe. Pushing her purse into the pocket of her jeans, she gave herself a quick, cursory glance in the mirror and stepped out on to the narrow landing, locking her door behind her.

Descending the three flights of stairs to the ground floor, she walked past the dining-room and through to the small reception area. Exchanging smiles with the girl behind the desk, she started to head for the hotel entrance and came to an abrupt halt, the colour flooding and then ebbing from her cheeks as she saw the tall figure sprawled idly in a chair just inside the door.

'Hello, Cassie.' Adam looked up from his newspaper, gave her a slow, lazy smile and rose unhurriedly to his feet.

'What are you doing here?' she blurted with total disbelief. She felt as if her legs were about to give way.

'Even professors take the occasional long weekend break,' he murmured mildly, folding up the newspaper and tossing it back on the chair.

And it was sheer coincidence of course that he'd just happened to select one of the lesser-known resorts in Switzerland for his break! She couldn't take her eyes from his face, devouring the familiar craggy male features rapaciously, warm, delighted pleasure flooding through her as her initial shock subsided. 'I didn't know you skied?' Her voice was far too high-pitched, unsteady.

'I don't,' he drawled.

'So you've just come for the bracing mountain air?' Her mouth curved, anticipation tingling down her spine as she waited for his answer.

'I've been lecturing in Lausanne the last couple of days.' He picked up his windproof jacket from the back of the chair and pulled it over his thick navy sweater. 'I bumped into Kate last week and told her I'd pop over and see you as I was going to be so close. See how you were getting on.'

Cassie's eyes slid from his face to the picture on the wall behind his head, the warm bubble bursting inside her, her brief illusion shattered. So it was coincidence after all that had brought Adam to Switzerland—and he'd only come to see her this morning as a favour to Kate. She must have overdone the life-is-wonderful routine in her letters home, and alerted Kate's suspicions that something was amiss.

'Well, you can report back that I'm fine. Having a terrific time,' she added enthusiastically.

'Are you?' The intent blue gaze searched her face.

'Of course,' she lied brightly. Averting her eyes swiftly, she glanced at her watch and let out a fake gasp of dismay. 'Good heavens, is that the time? I really must dash.' She zipped up her anorak and pulled her gloves from the pocket. 'How long are you staying in Saas?' She had no idea if he was booked in an hotel or merely come from Lausanne for the day. 'Perhaps we could meet for a chat and coffee later?' she added pleasantly. Good. That was just the right note of casual nonchalance. Friendly but unconcerned.

'I've hired a car for a couple of days and as it's your day off——' he smiled blandly, flicking a glance at the receptionist '—I checked . . . I wondered if you'd like to drive over to Zermatt. He opened the hotel door and followed her out into the street. 'See the Matterhorn.'

'Zermatt?' Cassie repeated, playing for time, uneasily conscious that her spirits were already spiralling upwards.

'Of course, if you've already made other plans for the day . . .' Adam shortened his stride to match hers.

'I suppose I could change them,' she murmured contemplatively as if reviewing her hectic schedule, but she knew that she'd already made her decision. If she'd known Adam was coming she could have prepared herself, but he'd caught her off guard, at her weakest and most vulnerable, and she simply didn't have the strength to refuse him. As long as she didn't start reading too much into the casual, friendly invitation, accepted it at face value, she would be safe enough, wouldn't she? Besides, she would be crazy to miss out on a chance to see the Matterhorn, she added, ignoring the warning bells in her head.

'Thank you, Adam. I'd love to go to Zermatt.' Pure, undiluted happiness tore through her as she glanced up at him, all her reservations disappearing. Nothing in the whole world mattered, except this moment, and the man with brilliant blue eyes smiling down into her upturned face. Tomorrow could take care of itself.

'I don't know where you put it all.' With mock bewilderment Adam surveyed Cassie over the top of his coffee-cup as, with a sigh of satisfaction, she finished her plate of apple strudel and custard.

'It's the mountain air,' she informed him with a grin. 'Besides, I only had a sandwich for lunch, not a huge plate of eggs and *rostis*,' she reminded him pointedly.

He grinned back at her and drained his cup. 'I think we ought to start walking back soon. It'll be dark in an hour.'

Cassie nodded in agreement. The lower route up to Zmutt, the tiny hamlet just above Zermatt, was well-trodden, the snow compact underfoot, but it would be all too easy to stray from the path in the dark and she didn't much fancy ending up in a snowdrift.

Adam turned his head, immediately caught the attention of a passing waitress, and requested their bill in fluent German.

The day had passed far too quickly, Cassie mused sadly, staring out of the window of the simple mountain restaurant from where the north east ridge of the Matterhorn was visible. A perfect day with the perfect companion.

Her eyes flicked back to Adam. He'd been good-humoured, entertaining and considerate. As they'd wandered around Zermatt earlier on, exploring the narrow traffic-free streets where fashionable boutiques, expensive jewellers and luxury hotels vied for space with old wooden chalets, she'd begun to relax, the constraint she'd felt in the car on the journey over slowly evaporating. She'd started to respond to Adam's gentle teasing, his light-hearted, impersonal conversation with increasing assurance. Except for her one brief enquiry about William, neither of them had referred to the past or to England. It was as if the day existed in a complete vacuum, a day stolen out of time with no yesterdays— and no tomorrows. Cassie shook herself mentally. No. She wasn't going to start thinking about the future and risk spoiling this blissful day. Whatever happened she would have these hours with Adam to treasure in her memory forever. Nothing could ever take that away from her.

'Ready?' Adam smiled across the checked tablecloth and she nodded, rising to her feet. He helped her on with her jacket, a courteous gesture that was as instinctive for him as opening the door for her.

Cassie stepped outside into the white world, her eyes protected from the glare of snow by sunglasses, and stood motionless, gazing up at the uniquely shaped mountain. She sensed Adam beside her but knew that he wouldn't break the spell, destroy the magic by uttering some trite observation, and in that shared moment of complete tranquillity she felt as close to him as if she were physically touching him. She tilted her head towards him and smiled. Then wordlessly they turned together and began the gradual descent to Zermatt.

'Careful, it's a bit slippery here,' Adam warned at one point, breaking the companionable easy silence.

Unselfconsciously, Cassie took hold of his proffered hand to steady herself, a wave of happiness fluttering through her as he made no attempt to release her hand, but kept it firmly clasped in his as they continued on down the path.

It suddenly seemed the most natural thing in the world to be walking hand in hand with Adam through the snow in the gathering dusk. She felt whole, complete, the void inside her filled. It was as if a part of her that had been missing had now been slotted back into place.

As they neared the outskirts of the once simple village that was now almost the size of a small town, Adam smiled down at her. 'I suppose you're hungry again?' he murmured with mock severity, his eyes teasing her.

'Well . . .' Cassie grinned back up at him, loving him so much in that moment that it was like a physical pain. 'Perhaps just a little snack?' she enquired hopefully. Anything to prolong this day that she never wanted to end.

The narrow streets were crowded with skiers returning from their day on the slopes, but Adam's height and breadth created an immediate pathway for them as he guided Cassie towards the town centre. With a swell of amusement, she observed the number of female heads that turned to appraise the man towering by her side, undisguised interest on their faces. Unable to resist, she flicked a sideways glance up at Adam but, if he was aware of the feminine attention he was commanding, he gave no indication of it. Perversely, it was that aloof indifference coupled with that undefinable air of complete self-assurance that made him even more compelling, singled him out in a street that was teeming with bronzed, vigorous, good-looking males.

They entered the bar of a *stubli* and Adam guided Cassie across the café to a table near the open log fire.

'*Raclette*?' Adam suggested as she sat down on a carved wooden chair, and she nodded her confirmation. Unobserved, her eyes moved over the strong profile as he ordered the cheese and potato dish together with a jug of Fendant, the local wine, from the waitress. As she listened to the deep, assured voice, a fierce rush of possessive pride tore through her. There would never be anyone to equal Adam. With a feeling of calm, sick inevitability she knew that she was going to spend the rest of her life searching for a man to measure up to him—and that she would fail.

She smiled absently as the waitress set a mat and cutlery in front of her and placed the jug of wine on the table.

'Have you enjoyed today?' Adam murmured, pouring wine into two small glasses.

'Yes,' she answered simply and was inordinately pleased to see the quiet satisfaction in his eyes.

'I suppose you're working tomorrow?'

She nodded, wondering if that note of regret in his voice had been her own wishful thinking. 'It's Saturday.

Change-over day.' The busiest day of the week. Her eyes dropped to her wine, her fingers curling around the glass. She didn't want to think about tomorrow... Didn't want to think about the loneliness that would invade her the moment she woke up in the morning, a loneliness that she knew now could only ever be assuaged by Adam.

'So when do you come back to England?'

'In about a month. In plenty of time to help Kate with the last-minute preparations for her wedding.'

'And then?' Adam prompted.

Cassie shrugged. She didn't want to talk about the future. Wanted just to enjoy the rest of the time she had left with Adam, to go on pretending for a little while longer that he was part of her life. 'I've been asked if I'd like to come back and work the summer season,' she said reluctantly.

'And would you like?' Adam asked casually, refilling her glass. 'Or do you plan going somewhere else?'

Cassie stared down into her glass. 'I think maybe I'll hang up my rucksack for a while.' The shadow in her eyes belied the flippancy in her voice. Wherever she travelled now she would always be wishing that Adam was by her side, would never be able to enjoy anything to the full without him. Resentment swelled up inside her at the realisation that he had that much power over her, could passively influence the whole course of her life. With miserable certainty she suddenly knew exactly what her future plans were going to be and they appalled her. She was going to return to Mead Cottage, work for Kate on a permanent basis... and spend every evening by the telephone just in case Adam should call, hold her breath every time she walked down the high street in case she bumped into him by chance. Oh, God, what a prospect, she thought bleakly.

'I'm glad.'

Slowly she lifted her eyes to him, her heart thudding as she saw the expression on his face.

'I've missed you like hell the last eight weeks,' he said quietly. 'I've been so damn miserable...'

Cassie froze. No. She didn't want to hear any of this. Didn't want to go through the agony of having her hopes raised and then dashed to the floor in pieces. She couldn't bear it, not again.

'Don't keep doing this to me, Adam. It's not f-fair.' Hardly aware of what she was doing, just giving in to that urgency to escape, she pushed back her chair and rose to her feet. Moving by the startled waitress who was approaching the table with the dishes of potato and melted cheese, she bolted towards the door.

She was halfway down the main street when Adam reached her. Ignoring her protests, he grabbed hold of her hand, his fingers clamping like a steel vice around her palm, and propelled her towards the railway station. In complete silence they boarded the waiting train to Tasche, the village just down the valley where they'd left the hire car.

Cassie sat by the window, staring out into the darkness, sick with misery. Was this how the perfect day was going to end? In a blank wall of angry, frigid silence? She shouldn't have rushed out of the café in the way she did, whatever the provocation, she thought with shame, wishing with all her heart she could put the clock back. She should have closed her ears to Adam's words, answered with some light-hearted quip, changed the subject somehow. Hell, why should she blame herself? He was the one at fault, pretending he cared about her, playing his callous game with her emotions...

She shot him a glance and flinched as she saw the expression on his face. She'd never seen him look so furious, could almost feel the iron self-control it was taking for him to keep the torrent of angry words in check. And then she understood. He was waiting until they were alone, away from any interested, curious observers, before giving full vent to his feelings...

The eruption finally came when they reached the hire car, parked a short distance away from the railway station at Tasche.

'What the hell was that all about?' he thundered, his eyes boring into her face like a drill.

She met the full force of his anger without flinching, facing him with icy composure. 'I shouldn't have walked out on you like that... I apologise. But I knew what you were going to say,' she continued levelly, 'and I didn't want to hear it.'

'You didn't want me to tell you I loved you?' His voice whipped through the air. 'Damn it, I know you care something for me. I can see it in your eyes, your face, hear it in your voice.' His eyes blazed down at her. 'Is this how you're going to spend the rest of your life? Running away from emotional involvement, commitment, terrified of loving or of being loved because of something that happened thirteen years ago?'

'What?' Cassie was too shocked to retaliate for a second and then the anger ignited again, seared through her. 'How can you talk about love, commitment?' she flared. 'You don't even know the meaning of the damn words.' How dared he imply she had some sort of hangup because of her rejection as a child? It wasn't true.

'You doubt me? Doubt I love you?' He sounded incredulous. 'Damn it all, Cassie. Have you any idea of what I've been through during the last two months? Any idea of the number of times I've booked a flight to Switzerland and then cancelled it? I had an open invitation to lecture in Lausanne, could have come at any time... by choice would have come during the summer... For Pete's sake, look at me...'

Slowly she raised her eyes to his again and then abruptly averted her head. 'Last time I thought...' she began in a strangled voice. 'And...' Her voice tailed off.

'And what?' he demanded forcefully.

'And all you wanted was a temporary c-casual affair...'

'There is nothing casual or temporary about the way I feel about you,' he exploded.

'But you told me that if it wasn't for William you'd ask me to move in with you——'

'I regretted that the minute I'd said it,' he cut in. 'I shouldn't have rushed things, should have taken everything more slowly. But I was impatient, wanted to see your reaction——' his mouth twisted bitterly '—and I certainly got it. The thought of even a hypothetical commitment scared you to death, sent you tearing off to Switzerland.'

'Me scared to death?' Cassie flung back at him. 'It was you who implied that all you wanted was——'

'Only because you looked so terrified at the very idea of living with me.'

'It wasn't the thought of living with you that terrified me...it was the idea of living without you...' It was too late to backtrack now, too late to think about pride. 'The thought of waking up one day and finding you'd tired of me... I just couldn't bear it...'

'Tire of you?' Adam muttered hoarsely. 'I want to spend the rest of my life with you...marry you.'

'What?' Cassie felt her head spinning as Adam pulled her into his arms. Please don't let this be another of his games, she thought with anguish.

'You will you marry me?' he demanded gruffly and, as Cassie searched his face, saw the vulnerability in his eyes, her heart squeezed, any last remaining doubt vanishing. Stretching up a hand, she touched his face.

'Yes, please,' she mumbled.

'Good.' His eyes glinted. 'I'd hate to disappoint my students.'

'Your students?' She eyed him suspiciously as he kissed her fingertips. Mmm. She'd never realised just how erogenous was the sensitive skin at the end of her fingers.

He smiled blandly. 'They seem to be under the impression that I'm about to trip down the aisle any day now, have been dropping heavy hints about wedding presents...'

'Susan?' Cassie lifted an eyebrow. That little episode seemed a lifetime away.

'I think that was when I first realised I wanted to marry you, although I didn't admit it to myself until a long time afterwards.' The corners of the straight mouth quirked. 'I rather liked the thought of you running around after me for the rest of your life...' Fending off her mock attack easily, he bent his head and gave her a long, lingering kiss.

'But why didn't you ask me sooner?' she enquired some time later, thinking of all the days and weeks of misery that could have been spared them both.

He gave a wry smile. '"Have rucksack, will travel",' he reminded her. 'Marriage didn't exactly appear to be on your agenda.' He paused. 'I kept convincing myself that I was protecting William, concerned that he might get too attached to you...when all the time I was protecting myself.' He touched her cheek lightly with his hand. 'Come on, get in the car before you freeze to death.'

Cassie walked around to the driver's side and then looked across the bonnet at Adam with complete bewilderment as he suddenly threw back his head and burst into laughter.

'We're in the Alps, amid some of the most beautiful, romantic scenery in the world—and where do I end up proposing to you? In the middle of a car park!'

Cassie grinned up at him inanely. Right now, this car park was the most beautiful place in the world.

'Richard's behaving like the proverbial mother hen,' Kate murmured, unconsciously pressing a hand to her abdomen. 'I think if he had his way he'd have me bed-ridden for the whole nine months.'

Cassie smiled back, thinking that she'd never seen her aunt look so serenely beautiful. 'More lemonade?' she enquired. They were seated in deck-chairs, beneath the shade of an old gnarled apple tree, watching William splash about in a plastic paddling pool.

As she picked up the jug to replenish the glasses, Lisa, sprawled by her feet, suddenly pricked up her ears and went charging up to the cottage.

'I think my husband's home.' Cassie grinned idiotically. My husband. She would never get tired of saying those two particular words. 'Back in a sec, Kate.'

Her bare, tanned legs covered the lawn in record time and she reached the back door in time to greet Adam.

'What's this, Professor?' she enquired severely as they entered the kitchen. 'Half-day?' He was currently lecturing at a summer school for Open University students.

'Had a pressing appointment,' he explained, and demonstrated with painstaking care exactly what that appointment was, kissing her soundly and with great thoroughness.

'Um, Adam,' Cassie murmured when she could breathe again. 'I'm going to have to defer my place at university again.' She'd applied and been accepted to read modern languages at the local university, the fact that she would be in a completely different department from Adam avoiding the inevitable problems that would otherwise arise. 'For at least five or six years anyway.' With great deliberation, Cassie stared out of the window at Kate's reclining form.

Adam frowned, and then his eyes darkened with comprehension and unconcealed delight. 'You're not...'

'I am.'

'Quick... A chair...'

'I don't need to sit down,' she assured him with an ecstatic smile. 'I'm not an invalid.'

'You might not need to sit down, but I do,' he informed her loftily, lowering himself on to a stool and pulling her on to his lap. 'It's not every day I learn that I'm going to be a father. In fact——' the blue eyes moved with ill-concealed joy over her face '—I think it's the first time in my life.'

'I should think so too,' Cassie said primly and then, curling her hands through his hair, began to kiss him in a manner that was far from prim.

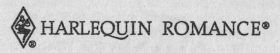 **HARLEQUIN ROMANCE®**

brings you

More Romances Celebrating Love, Families and Children!

Following on from Rosemary Gibson's *No Ties*, Harlequin Romance #3344, this month we're bringing you *A Valentine for Daisy*, Harlequin Romance #3347, which we know you will enjoy reading! It's a wonderful Betty Neels story, all about two adorable twins Josh and Katie who play their part in Daisy finding true love at last!

Watch out for these titles:

KIDSG9

Fifty red-blooded, white-hot, true-blue hunks
from every State in the Union!

Look for MEN MADE IN AMERICA! Written by some
of our most popular authors, these stories feature some
of the strongest, sexiest men, each from a different state
in the union!

Two titles available every month at your favorite
retail outlet.

In January, look for:

WITHIN REACH by Marilyn Pappano (New Mexico)
IN GOOD FAITH by Judith McWilliams (New York)

In February, look for:

THE SECURITY MAN by Dixie Browning
(North Carolina)
A CLASS ACT by Kathleen Eagle
(North Dakota)

You won't be able to resist MEN MADE IN AMERICA!

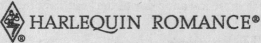

HARLEQUIN ROMANCE®

Starting in March, we are bringing you a brand-new
series—Sealed with a Kiss. We've all written SWAK at
some time on a love letter, and in these books the love
story always concerns a letter—one way or another!

We've chosen RITA nominee Leigh Michaels's
Invitation to Love (Harlequin Romance #3352)
as the first title and will be bringing you one
every month, right through to Christmas!

Watch for *Invitation to Love* by Leigh Michaels in March.
And don't miss any of these exciting **Sealed with a Kiss**
titles, by your favorite Harlequin Romance authors:

April	#3355	Dearest Love	Betty Neels
May	#3360	P.S. I Love You	Valerie Parv
June	#3366	Mail-Order Bridegroom	Day Leclaire
July	#3370	Wanted: Wife and Mother	Barbara McMahon

Available wherever Harlequin books are sold.

On the most romantic day of the year, capture the thrill of falling in love all over again—with

Harlequin's

Bachelors

They're three sexy and *very single* men who run very special personal ads to find the women of their fantasies by Valentine's Day. These exciting, passion-filled stories are written by bestselling Harlequin authors.

Your Heart's Desire by Elise Title
Mr. Romance by Pamela Bauer
Sleepless in St. Louis by Tiffany White

Be sure not to miss Harlequin's Valentine Bachelors, available in February wherever Harlequin books are sold.

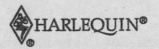

Bestselling Author

Elise Title

Anything less than everything is not enough.

Coming in January 1995, Sylver Cassidy and Kate Paley take on the movers and shakers of Hollywood. Young, beautiful, been-there, done-it-all type women, they're ready to live by their own rules and stand by their own mistakes. With love on the horizon, can two women bitten by the movie bug really have it all? Find out in

HOT
PROPERTY

HARLEQUIN®

Don't miss these Harlequin favorites by some of our most
distinguished authors!
And now, you can receive a discount by ordering two or more titles!

HT#25577	WILD LIKE THE WIND by Janice Kaiser	$2.99	☐
HT#25589	THE RETURN OF CAINE O'HALLORAN by JoAnn Ross	$2.99	☐
HP#11626	THE SEDUCTION STAKES by Lindsay Armstrong	$2.99	☐
HP#11647	GIVE A MAN A BAD NAME by Roberta Leigh	$2.99	☑
HR#03293	THE MAN WHO CAME FOR CHRISTMAS by Bethany Campbell	$2.89	☐
HR#03308	RELATIVE VALUES by Jessica Steele	$2.89	☐
SR#70589	CANDY KISSES by Muriel Jensen	$3.50	☐
SR#70598	WEDDING INVITATION by Marisa Carroll	$3.50 U.S.	☐
		$3.99 CAN.	☐
HI#22230	CACHE POOR by Margaret St. George	$2.99	☐
HAR#16515	NO ROOM AT THE INN by Linda Randall Wisdom	$3.50	☐
HAR#16520	THE ADVENTURESS by M.J. Rodgers	$3.50	☐
HS#28795	PIECES OF SKY by Marianne Willman	$3.99	☐
HS#28824	A WARRIOR'S WAY by Margaret Moore	$3.99 U.S.	☐
		$4.50 CAN.	☐

(limited quantities available on certain titles)

	AMOUNT	$
DEDUCT:	**10% DISCOUNT FOR 2+ BOOKS**	$
ADD:	**POSTAGE & HANDLING**	$
	($1.00 for one book, 50¢ for each additional)	
	APPLICABLE TAXES*	$_____
	TOTAL PAYABLE	$_____
	(check or money order—please do not send cash)	

To order, complete this form and send it, along with a check or money order for the
total above, payable to Harlequin Books, to: **In the U.S.:** 3010 Walden Avenue,
P.O. Box 9047, Buffalo, NY 14269-9047; **In Canada:** P.O. Box 613, Fort Erie, Ontario,
L2A 5X3.

Name: _____

Address: _____ City: _____

State/Prov.: _____ Zip/Postal Code: _____

*New York residents remit applicable sales taxes.
 Canadian residents remit applicable GST and provincial taxes.

HBACK-JM2